Ernst Wilhelm von Brücke

The Human Figure

Its Beauties and Defects

Ernst Wilhelm von Brücke

The Human Figure
Its Beauties and Defects

ISBN/EAN: 9783337366230

Printed in Europe, USA, Canada, Australia, Japan

Cover: Foto ©Andreas Hilbeck / pixelio.de

More available books at **www.hansebooks.com**

THE HUMAN FIGURE:

ITS BEAUTIES AND DEFECTS.

BY

ERNST BRÜCKE,

EMERITUS PROFESSOR OF PHYSIOLOGY IN THE UNIVERSITY OF VIENNA,
AND FORMERLY TEACHER OF ANATOMY IN THE ACADEMY
OF FINE ARTS AT BERLIN.

WITH A PREFACE,

BY

WILLIAM ANDERSON,

*Professor of Anatomy to the Royal Academy of Arts, London, and Lecturer on
Anatomy at St. Thomas's Hospital.*

AUTHORISED TRANSLATION, REVISED BY THE AUTHOR.

With 29 Illustrations by Hermann Paar.

LONDON:

H. GREVEL & CO.,

33, KING STREET, COVENT GARDEN, W.C.

1891.

CONTENTS.

PREFACE.

THE learned author of "Schönheit und Fehler der menschlichen Gestalt" requires little introduction either to the scientific or to the artistic world in this country, for his name has been closely associated with the progress of human physiology in all its branches for upwards of forty years, and during the whole of his professional career he has applied much of his knowledge and power of research to the elucidation of questions of art. His love for art—doubtless an inheritance from his father, who was a distinguished painter of portraits and historical pictures—was brought into service as early as 1846, when he was elected teacher of anatomy in the Akademie der Künste, in Berlin ; and since this time his innumerable contributions to scientific literature have been interspersed with important essays bearing upon the subject of his predilections. His " Physiologie der Farben für die Zwecke der Kunstgewerbe bearbeitet " and " Bruchstücke aus der Theorie der

bildenden Künste " are well known and esteemed,
and his latest work, of which the translation is now
before us, gives in clear, untechnical style the outcome of his ripe experience and close reflection upon
a topic which should appeal, not only to the student
of art, but to every one who desires to gain an insight
into the philosophy of human beauty.

The object of the volume is given by the author
in the opening of his preface. He addresses himself
both to artists and to amateurs,—" to the former, in
order to draw their attention to many things which,
we know from experience, they not infrequently
overlook ; and to the latter, in order to introduce to
them a way of studying works of art which, although
not habitually pursued by the amateur, is nevertheless
indispensable to the proper understanding and due
appreciation of them."   For the amateur, indeed,
the indications offered in his pages are of especial
interest.   Most persons cherish a secret conviction
of their capacity to arbitrate on any question of
personal beauty,—a fond belief that is not at all
disturbed by the knowledge that in any particular
case their friends will arrive with equal self-satis-
faction at conclusions of a different kind,—but there
are few who are prepared to advance cogent reasons
for the faith that is in them.   There must, indeed,

be two factors in the ability to form a sound judgment,—the innate sense of beauty of line and surface which perhaps all possess, but in very different degrees; and a regulated comparative study, for which Professor Brücke here furnishes a guide, of the best examples in nature and art. A liberal endowment with the first—a natural and often inherited qualification—of course lightens and fructifies the labour involved in the attainment of the second, but both are equally essential for the qualification of the true critic.

It will be noticed that our author, who desires to spare his lay readers as far as possible, has been unable to avoid altogether the introduction of anatomical details, and this is sufficient to prove that some acquaintance with the science is desirable for those who would follow his system. Nevertheless, it is certain that anatomy, unless studied from the æsthetic aspect, is of little use. An anatomist may be no more competent to give a verdict upon a question of the beautiful than a person who has never heard the name of a single muscle in his body; for we know that learned authors of anatomical text-books will sometimes without a qualm admit pictorial illustrations to their own writings that are as painful to the artistic sense as a false note to the ear of the

musician.   On the other hand, such a familiarity
with the human figure as may be gleaned by casual
and unreflecting inspection is of no greater value.   It
has often been asserted that the marvellous achieve-
ments of the ancient Greeks in sculpture were a
result of their daily opportunities of seeing the nude
form ; but this theory is by no means satisfactory.
Some other nations, gifted with strong artistic
instincts, have possessed the same advantages, and
have derived no such benefit from them : the
Japanese, for example, have had continually before
them in their daily life types of manly and womanly
beauty, which, if not quite in accordance with
European ideals of perfection, are still worthy to
inspire the painter or sculptor ; and yet, although
this people will manifest in their delineation of a
flower, a bird, a monkey, or a fish, an unsurpassed
appreciation of grace and veracity, their renderings
of human life are, from the academical point of
view, little better than caricatures.   An illustration
of the same principle has just been afforded to me
by a friend who has had the portrait of a favourite
hunter painted by a local *pictor ignotus*.   He believes
it to be an admirable representation, and theoreti-
cally his opinion should be conclusive, for he has
been associated with horses all his life, and is

regarded as a good judge of the points of the animal ; but had he studied the equine form as Professor Brücke teaches us to study the form of a man or woman, he would have detected in the effigy a score of gross errors of outline and proportion of which both he and the painter now rest in happy unconsciousness.

For the higher successes in artistic presentment of the nude a knowledge of the skeleton, joints, and muscles must always be of the greatest importance. It is not necessary that the painter or sculptor should attack such a mass of detail as the student of medicine is called upon to prepare for the satisfaction of his examiners,—most of this would be useless drudgery,—but, on the other hand, there are features to which the future surgeon or physician devotes no attention that for the artist will give a meaning to every line that he draws or surface that he models, a meaning that may not be patent to all, but that will be appreciated by those who are educated to look for the intellectual as well as for the imitative faculty in a work of art. There are artists who have maintained that all scientific accomplishment is superfluous in the exercise of their calling, and who have lived down to the creed, but their mistake is demonstrated both by the history of art and by the internal evidence afforded by its greatest monuments ;

for beauty in art is only well-selected, well-com-
prehended, and well-expressed truth, and science is
the glass which enables us to recognise and estimate
truths that are hidden from or but dimly conjectured
by the unaided vision of ignorance. The wisdom of
Ecclesiastes has said it, " The wise man is he who
knoweth the interpretation of things."

We do not know how the consummate science
of Pheidias was acquired. That he was a perfect
master of the superficial forms of anatomy can be
doubted by no expert who has studied the marvellous
relics of his genius that Mr. Frederic Harrison
proposes to restore to classic soil ; but it is im-
probable that he received the same kind of training
that was sought nearly twenty centuries later by
Leonardo da Vinci in his association with the
physician Marcantonio della Torre, and by Michelangelo with Realdo Colombo ; for the Greek sculptor
lived before the school of Alexandria had opened
the way for direct anatomical research by dissection
of the human subject, and we know, moreover, that
Hippocrates, his great medical contemporary, who,
we must believe, would gladly have availed himself
of any opportunities that were possible, had but the
crudest ideas upon the structure of the body. When,
however, we pass from the age of Pericles to the age

of Lorenzo de' Medici, a clearer light shines upon the artist and his methods of learning, and we find that painting and sculpture went hand in hand with the practical study of anatomy, and that the greatest masters were those most profoundly versed in anatomical detail. It would be easy to fill a volume with the history of the service rendered by artists to anatomy and by anatomists to art, but this is not the place to attempt such a task; and it must be enough to say that the story would only strengthen the position taken by the author of the work before us.

In conclusion, a word of appreciation should be given for the beautiful specimens of wood engraving executed for the author by Herr Hermann Paar. It should perhaps be pointed out that most of the anatomical drawings, although directly borrowed, as is duly acknowledged in the text, from Hollstein's "Anatomie des Menschen," are really English in origin, and are copies from the vigorous and accurate woodcuts of the brothers Bagge in Wilson's "Anatomists' Vade-Mecum."

WILLIAM ANDERSON.

INTRODUCTION.

THE following pages are addressed to artists and to amateurs : to the former, in order to draw their attention to many things which, as we know from experience, they not infrequently overlook ; and to the latter, in order to introduce to them a way of studying works of art which, though not habitually pursued by amateurs, is nevertheless indispensable for the proper understanding and due appreciation of them. There is a general consensus of opinion, saving that of a few, among living artists, that the graphic and plastic arts have sunk from the level they formerly maintained—painting even more so than sculpture ; and nowhere is the fact more manifest than in Italy, the great treasure-house of the Arts. The history of painting in that country may be divided into four periods : that of the newly-awakened art, when the painters strove after high ideals, but could as yet achieve little ; the period of splendour, in which the masterly character of the execution corresponded to the lofty nature of the ideal ; the period of decline, when the ideal aimed at had ceased to have any value, though the painters were still masters of their craft ;

and, lastly, a fourth period, one without a name, when not only had the ideals ceased to have any value, but the artists' hands had lost their cunning.

And yet are not the Italians as gifted now as in the fifteenth and sixteenth centuries? Does not the spirit which they breathe into certain branches of industrial art clearly show it? And is it not proved by some of their modern works of sculpture, which shine like lonely stars in a wilderness of unintelligent, nay, inconceivable, rubbish? *

The causes of the decline of the fine arts are of divers kinds. They cannot all be enumerated here, and some are not of a nature to admit of being over-come. No reasonable person believes it possible for the men of our day, arrayed in frock-coats, trousers, and tall hats, to have an art such as was theirs who lived in ancient times, or even in the fifteenth and sixteenth centuries. But it is possible to fight against some errors, and it is the purpose of these pages to combat erroneous tendencies in the representation of the human body.

The realism which dominates all art at the present day is so interpreted by many of our artists that they rate the results of their labour in proportion to the accuracy with which they can reproduce the model. Every detail, be it beautiful or the reverse, is copied, in order to ward off the charge of being "conventional." And yet how dangerous is this slavish copying of the model! It is dangerous enough on

* As I once heard an Italian himself describe it—"*Roba!*"

the other side of the Alps, but on this side it is even
more so.   Northern sculptors who have passed a
considerable time in Rome, and have executed works
there deserving of praise for nobleness and refinement
of form, in a few years after returning to their own
country frequently degenerate in a marked degree ;
their forms grow coarse, and blemishes crop up which
occur much more often in the bodily structure of
Northerns than in that of Italians.   This is the effect
of adhering to the model.   When standing before the
living subject we tolerate much that the cold marble
may not offer to our gaze.   Let me be forgiven for
making a somewhat base comparison : the artist
ought to know the defects of the human body just
as a judge of horseflesh knows the weak points in the
build of a horse. He need not on that account be
monotonous, or make all his figures conform to a
conventional standard ; but he will seek for beauty
in all her divers manifestations.

What, then, is the beauty of which we speak?   I
would define that figure as beautiful which can be
displayed to advantage in any position and under
any aspect that occurs in ideal art.

I have adopted a purely artistic standpoint in
making beauty depend, not on the subjective sense
of pleasure at the sight of any given object, but on a
much more definite factor, viz., a general conformity
to the demands of ideal art.   Much has been written
about sensuous beauty and the beauty of sensuousness ;
but where sensuousness has been sought for its own

sake it has brought more harm than good. For to
this element it is owing that in the incipient decline
of Italian art the nobler ideals of female beauty gave
way to lower ones, and that at the present day painters
and sculptors take so little heed of the defects of their
female models.

As I have already remarked, a figure, to be beautiful
in our sense, must be capable of being displayed to
advantage in all positions and under all aspects which
present themselves in ideal art.   This means, moreover,
that in any position occurring in ideal art, and under
any aspect, the figure must yield harmonious lines ; for
the ordering of the lines of the composition is the
point of primary importance in every work of art that
claims to be judged by a high standard.   The fact
that in recent times the feeling for beauty of line has
fallen so much into neglect—one might almost venture
to affirm that it is only to be found in isolated instances—involves a grave reproach to modern art, as
compared with that of antiquity and the renaissance.
It is the outlines of the features which determine the
general impression made by the face, and which stamp
it with their own character, rendering it clear or con-
fused, noble or ignoble, as the case may be.   How else
were it possible to produce such effects as we see
produced by means of mere outlines, without a trace
of shading?   Even in favourable instances no impression of actual bodily presence can equal the trenchant
effect brought about by simple lines, not even in
Nature herself.   This is demonstrated by the familiar

fact that the portrait painter shifts his model so as to obtain more or less of the full face or profile, according as he thinks thereby to arrive at the most satisfactory picture. Many a head which produces quite a charming effect when seen in full face would, if painted in profile, belong to the category of things not to be tolerated. Indeed, were we as directly and immediately conscious of the differences of plane of the third dimension, *i.e.*, that of depth, as we are of the outlines which fall on the retina, we should in such instances experience an equally disagreeable impression from the full-face portrait as from the profile.

I have purposely insisted on variety in position and aspect, since it is possible for a great master so to handle even models which leave much to be desired, as to compel an acknowledgment of the harmony of their lines. Rubens is a striking instance of this. His models, children apart, are almost invariably of a common type, especially his women. These are plump Flemish girls between twenty and thirty years of age. Sometimes the coarseness of his models ruins the picture, as, for instance, in his Three Graces, which move us only to laughter or disgust. Sometimes, however, his genius conquers all obstacles, as in the Nymph of Diana (according to some, Diana herself), who carries a spear in her right hand and on her left arm the spoils of the chase, and is accompanied by her hounds, while a faun, bearing fruits of the field, goes before her. Here details which would be coarse, or perhaps repulsive, in the model are not shown ;

the lines, regarded in relation to the subject and the
surroundings, are perfect, and there is no denying
them a certain spirit, and even greatness. But success
in such a case only justifies the artist, not the model.
No one ever knew so well as Michelangelo Buonarroti
how to produce powerful and strangely harmonious
effects by means of figures in themselves open to
criticism, simply by his mode of placing and ordering
them and of distributing their lines. For him a
figure existed only in his particular representation
of it ; how it would have looked in any other position
was a matter of no concern to him. On this account,
and not merely by reason of any necessary failure
all round, did the tendency to imitate, or even go
beyond, Michelangelo, prove so fatal to artists of a
lesser calibre. The ancients acted in a wholly different fashion. The sculptors of antiquity endeavoured
to produce the most beautiful Venus, Apollo, Juno,
or Minerva possible. If we placed the Venus of
Milo or the Venus de Medici in the position of the
Ariadne, they would still be as beautiful as before ;
the Crouching Venus might raise herself to her full
height without suffering any disparagement ; nay,
more, their nude forms are frequently placed, inten-   ·
tionally it would seem, in attitudes which demand a
beauty absolutely without blemish.

As artists are not unfamiliar with anatomy, I
have combined anatomical considerations, so far as I
deemed it desirable, with criticism of the external
form. We moderns, who are no longer in a position

to stamp the human form on our minds by daily and hourly contemplation of it, are driven to rely on our anatomical knowledge to guide us among the manifold variations of structure with which we have to deal. If the anatomist should find that here and there details have been simplified or treated somewhat diagrammatically, let him put it down to the purpose of this work. No one knows better than an anatomist like myself that perfect insight can only be gained by studying the dead subject scalpel in hand ; but I have preferred to sacrifice some detail to my aim of instilling correct general notions rather than expose myself to the danger of being difficult to understand.

I

THE HEAD AND NECK.

NO part of the human body has given rise to more diverse opinions as to what should be accounted beautiful than the head, and more especially the face. And this is only natural, seeing that here so profound an influence is exerted by character and expression.

Since in this volume we are dealing exclusively with their representation in art, differences of opinion as to individual faces or reproductions of them are of subordinate significance, compared with the important fact that sculpture and painting differ essentially in their respective modes of appealing to us. Apart from the influence which colour as such exercises on the spectator, the difference arises from the fact that the eyes, which convey so much meaning in a picture, lose the main part of their force in a statue or bust. Moreover, the sculptor must aim at making the head effective from whatever side it is viewed, while the painter is satisfied if he can find but one good aspect —that, namely, which he proposes to reproduce. The sculptor must further endeavour to embody forms which, in every change of light and every alteration of the point of view, shall, by a proper distribution of light and shade, present under all circumstances and equally at a distance the prominent features and characteristic lines of the face. I say advisedly by a proper distribution of light and shade, because the distance at which works of sculpture are seen is usually too considerable to allow of our effectually employing the means afforded us, by the movements of our eyes, of accurately estimating the gradations of the third dimension—that of depth. The differences of depth presented by the human face are too insignificant when seen at a distance.*

Such are the considerations which controlled the growth of the ideals of the Greek sculptors, ideals which will never fade so long as plastic art exists. The lines which they follow are familiar to us.

The forehead, or at least that portion of it which is left uncovered by the hair, is usually rather low. The eyebrows are well arched, and pass without a break at the root of the nose into the border-lines of its bridge. This is essential, firstly, for the production of a good profile, on account of the line leading from

---

* We perceive objects with our eyes singly, that is, at one and the same point of the field of vision, since the image is formed on the centre of the retina in both eyes at the so-called yellow spot, or *fovea centralis*. Therefore the axis of the eye passing through the latter point must be directed at the object. When this happens simultaneously in both eyes, the angle which the two axes make with one another becomes smaller as the distance of the object increases, and for objects at an infinite distance the angle ceases to exist, *i.e.*, the two axes

the forehead to the bridge of the nose; secondly, by reason of the way in which the eyes are seen when viewed from the side or in so-called three-quarter view; and, in the third place, because by this means the shadows are so distributed, that even in full face and at a considerable distance the continuity of the nose with the forehead is maintained. Thus the line passing from the eyebrows to the nose is marked as we are accustomed to draw it in outline drawings.

The bridge of the nose is straight and flush with the forehead, not set at an angle to it, nor separated from it by a depression. This is essential to the noble simplicity of the antique type, which was designed to produce its effect equally when seen in strict profile.

The eye is set horizontally, and not in a line running obliquely from above in a downward and inward direction. Since this feature has so often been insisted on, I must observe that a slight rise in the line of the eyes has not in all periods been regarded as ugly. We find such eyes in the works of the early

are parallel. As the distance diminishes, the angle increases in size, very slowly so long as the distance is great; when the object approaches so near that the distance between the two eyes themselves is no longer very minute in proportion to the distance of the object, the angle grows rapidly larger. For this reason, when the distance is considerable, perceptions of depth and range, that is, of larger or smaller distances from the observer's eye, are by no means accurate unless light and shade come to the assistance of our perceptive faculties.

Italian masters, who had not as yet studied the antique, and who in developing the art they inherited from the Byzantines took their own course. Giotto and his followers offer numerous examples, even in instances where they are endeavouring to portray figures of ideal beauty. The frescoes ascribed to Orcagna in Sta. Maria Novella, at Florence, prove convincingly that a noble and touching type of beauty is compatible with a moderately oblique position of the eyes. In these instances the deviation from what we regard as the artistic norm is not so much in the direction of the arch of the brow as in that of the aperture of the eye, which bends up towards the temples more than is the case in works of art of the mature renaissance.

The horizontal position of the eye-slit among the ancients has been more often insisted on than the circumstance that the outer angle of the eye is usually carried farther backwards, in comparison with the inner angle, than is the case in the majority of living people we meet with. This has the advantage of showing the eye better in profile. Of course it has no influence on the direction of the line of sight, in the physiological sense of the phrase, on the optic axes—*i.e.*, straight lines drawn from the object observed to the central points of the two eyes. These lines are, under all circumstances, dependent on the position of the object on which the gaze of the eyes is fixed. It is merely that a larger portion of the eyeball is visible within the eyelids when seen from the side.

The eyelids of a sculptor's model, especially the
upper one, should not have too thin a border, and
the horizontal surface of the border should be sharply
divided off from the vertical surface. The aid which
the eyelashes render to the painter in drawing the
eye is denied to the sculptor. When the eye is wide
open, the eyelid should be separated from the ridge
of the brow by a simple and well-arched line, unen-
cumbered by irregular secondary folds. If the eye
is cast down, the line descending in profile from the
prominence of the brow to the point of the eyelid
corresponding to the centre of the cornea should be
straight and unbroken. During sleep the cornea is
directed upwards, and its position should be indicated
by a faint elevation of the eyelid.

The cheek-bones must not be too prominent, and
the surface of the cheek should pass evenly without
interruption into that of the upper lip. This is the
rule in antique works representing ideal female
beauty or the heads of beautiful youths. The line,
occurring so frequently amongst ourselves, which takes
its origin just outside the nostril at its upper corner,
and, making a curve round the corner of the mouth,
ends there, is found only in figures of aged individuals and of satyrs, and in laughing figures. To
reproduce it in a face making a claim to ideal beauty
is a blunder which modern art, in its slavish imitation
of the model, unhappily does not always succeed in
avoiding. For we have among us a large proportion
of young and good-looking girls in whom this line

is well marked, and thus artists are misled into reproducing it.

This line, when not the result of age or of facial contortion produced by laughing, is caused by prominence of the cheek-bones, by excessive width of the upper row of teeth as measured from the anterior molars of one side to those of the other, or else by the teeth being set obliquely with their crowns jutting forwards and outwards, and their fangs retreating inwards. These factors may act singly or together ; and, further, the consistency of the fleshy parts, an insufficiently tense skin, or the distribution of the fat, may take some share in it.

A restricted width of the palate, measured between the molars of each side, forms an important factor in the beauty of a head in yet another respect. It stands in correlation with a modest span of lower jaw, which thus is able to pass over into the neck without the intervention of a strong ridge, so that the surface of the cheek lying between the corner of the mouth and the ear may be continued into the lateral surface of the neck without any excessive accumulation of fat in the latter. A similar narrowness of the palate may be observed even more strikingly shown in the Dying Adonis in the Bargello at Florence, ascribed to Michelangelo, than in most antique sculptures.

A mouth which is to serve the sculptor as a model of beauty should display the characteristic lines which we see in the antique, and the border-line between the skin and the red part of the lips should be distinctly marked by their contour, and not by the colour only. A model who does not show this, and in whom, though the lips and adjacent skin are distinguished by colour, the contour of the mouth is indistinct or unpleasing, is useless to the sculptor and an unfavourable subject for the painter.

The lips of the closed mouth must be so adjusted that the line of division between them is marked by a deep shadow along its entire length from one angle of the mouth to the other. The sculptor will frequently have recourse to a deepening of the groove in order to emphasize the line of division. Partly with this object, and partly for the sake of the expression, it was a practice, even in classical times, for the sculptor to leave the mouth slightly open. The line of the closed mouth should form two waves moving to meet one another, with their descending parts in the centre. The notch so formed may be more 'or less rounded. The form of the wave is subject to a considerable range of variation ; but where the wave is non-existent, giving place to a mere arch or a straight line, such a mouth is of no use to the sculptor. The slightly-opened mouth should not terminate laterally in sharp angles, but should be bounded on each side by a line running from above in a downward and outward direction.

It is notorious that in many antiques the point of attachment of the ears is placed higher than that ordinarily occurring in the living subject, and this has been quoted as evidence for deriving Greek from Egyptian art; but C. Langer ("Anatomie der äusseren Formen des menschlichen Körpers," Vienna, 1884) has observed, quite accurately, that this phenomenon is by no means of universal occurrence in archaic statues, and that in one of the best known, the Apollo of Tenea, the ears are correctly set on the head.

The chin in the antique is rounded, often with a slight median depression, and with the most convex part of its surface directed less obliquely backward and more forward than in most of the living faces we see around us.

The antique type of face is regarded by many as an ideal form which is not to be found at the present day, and perhaps never existed at all; but an attentive observer may succeed in meeting with heads in Italy, and occasionally even in Germany, which approach this ideal very closely; and I am informed by an excellent artist, who has lived for a long time in the East, that the type may be met with in Smyrna in its purest form.

It is worthy of remark that the aquiline nose, which is by no means of rare occurrence in Italy, never found any acceptance in relation to female beauty among the artists of the middle ages and renaissance. When they do deviate from the Greek profile, they tend to make the bridge of the nose no longer join the forehead by a straight line; but where they alter the form of the nose itself, they never do it so as to convert it into an aquiline nose.

Indeed, they rather fall into the opposite tendency; and in the early renaissance period we not infrequently, in the heads of women or angels making claim to ideal beauty, meet with noses which fall considerably behind the antique in size. They are not, of course, set on Greek heads, but are co-ordinated with a childlike type of countenance.

In Raffaelle's pictures several heads are alleged to be portraits of the Fornarina. The master is, however, made responsible for marked deviations from the original, if the female portrait in the Barberini Gallery at Rome, bearing the signature of Raffaelle on the armlet, really represents the Fornarina. None of the heads of the Fornarina so-called in his other pictures has the accentuated aquiline nose of the girl depicted there.

In the autumn of 1882 I saw in the Pinacoteca at Lucca a Madonna which resembled the Fornarina portrait more closely than any other I know of, but the nose was less strongly marked. The Madonna did not form part of the collection, but was stated to be the property of a Contessa Nobili. By some it was regarded as a work of Raffaelle, but by others was attributed to Giulio Romano.

It has often been asserted that the ancients had smaller heads than the existing race of men; and, according to the ordinary methods of measurement, this is in the main correct. These methods have certain practical advantages for artists when at work; but it is not scientifically correct to compare the

height of the whole figure with the so-called height
of the head, because thereby the quotient is strongly
affected by the considerable range of variation in the
length of the legs. Now, among the moderns the
legs are often shorter than among the ancients, as
represented in their art. If, then, we were to compare the height of the head in the living subject
with the height of the trunk only as measured from
the top of the scalp to the pubic region, we should
arrive at a result much more like that furnished
by measurements of the antique.

A second cause of the difference just mentioned
is the more extensive development of the facial skull
among the barbarian races whose descendants form
a preponderant majority of the present population
of Europe. The artist has to distinguish between the
facial skull and the cerebral skull, or brain-case, as
the development of the two by no means coincides,
and is the result of two different sets of causes. The
brain-case determines the shape of the upper part of
the head. If a line be drawn from the root of the
nose through the eye and the aperture of the ear,
—that is, the entrance of the external auditory
meatus,—and thence to the bony ridge in the occipital
region, which may be distinguished on each side
by the finger from the muscles and ligaments
which are attached thereto, all that lies above this
line forms the brain-case, and all below it the facial
skull ; and in the latter it is mainly the greater
development of the jaw which concerns us. In the

upper jaw it is an increase of its height that adds to the dimension of the height of the head ; in the lower jaw the projection of it in a downward direction, occasioned either by its size or by its oblique position.

If the line above described be drawn on modern profile portraits copied accurately from life, and on profile portraits from the antique, the difference will frequently be perceptible, especially if a perpendicular line be drawn from the aperture of the ear towards the neck.

C. Rochet lays it down that in a beautiful profile head the distance of the aperture of the ear, or of the tragus covering it, from the chin should not exceed its distance from the scalp; a proportion that is found oftener in the antique than in life. He also asserts that the Romans had the smallest under-jaw. His studies on this subject are to be found in a lecture delivered before the Anthropological Society of Paris, on November 29th, 1866.

At the same time, among the Greeks, too, the brain-case seems usually not to have been large, and the high-arched crown of the head now so often met with would seem not to have been of frequent occurrence, to judge by the portrait statues that have come down to us. That art, when it has a free choice, should not reproduce it is not wonderful. It should be mentioned here that the Venus of the Esquiline, an antique work of art of great beauty, has proportionately a large head one which would not look at all too small on the shoulders of a living girl.

The neck in antique female portraits approaches a cylindrical shape more closely than in most living persons ; and, indeed, amongst the latter, the more even its rounded surface is, the more beautiful it is deemed. In many antiques which have the head slightly bent forwards, so that the neck is inclined rather obliquely in a backward and downward direction, its shape is strikingly cylindrical, its girth at the top scarcely differing from that at its base. It must be admitted, however, that the antero-posterior diameter is somewhat longer than the transverse diameter.

The following rough-and-ready rule may serve in the choice of a model : When the neck is at once thin and cylindrical, it is beautiful ; when it is cylindrical and likewise thick, it may be very ugly, but even uglier when it is thin and yet not cylindrical. For when it is thick its cylindrical shape may be due to a somewhat excessive layer of fat ; and when it is thin, but not cylindrical, this condition may arise from excessive leanness. This rule, of course, does not entitle the artist to make the neck as thin and cylindrical as he chooses, but applies solely to the choice of a model. Nature herself takes care to keep within the limits which the artist should respect.

It is sometimes laid down that the circumference of the neck should be equal to that of the calf of the leg at its widest part, but this is incorrect. The neck, when free from all swellings,* remains always more or less behind the calf in size in individuals with a well-developed muscular system.   In the Sleeping Ariadne of the Vatican the neck, to judge by the eye merely, is scarcely thicker than the upper arm.   The proportion which the artist has adopted in this case certainly deviates from what we ordinarily find in youthful figures of similar build to the Ariadne, but it is not beyond the range of possibility.

In a living model, who is otherwise well-fitted for the representation of an ideal figure, such a condition may, in general, be regarded as an advantage, as in such a case the neck is sure not to be too thin for the rest of the body, nor the upper arm too thick, provided, as we have said, that the rest of the body is suitable for an ideal figure.

Anteriorly the neck is bounded below on each side by the line of the clavicles, or more accurately by a line running above the clavicles, which should not themselves be visible.   Behind, it slopes away on each side into the contours leading from the neck to the shoulders.   Apart from modifications caused by the presence of more or less fat, these contours are determined, in the first place, by the superior fibres of the trapezius muscle (*Musculus cucullaris* or *trapezius*) and their state of contraction, and, secondly, by the

---

* Swellings of the thyroid body, and a swollen condition of the deeper veins of the neck, are constantly met with in certain districts, and may easily pass unperceived by the untrained observer.

muscles lying beneath them and their points of attachment to the skeleton. The girls and women of the Romagna are famed for the beauty of these lines and of the attachment of the neck to the shoulders. Cylindrical necks resembling the antique I have frequently seen in Tuscany.

Furthermore, the line defining the contour where the neck merges into the shoulder, when viewed from the front, deserves special consideration. As already mentioned, it is determined in the first place, apart from the fat layer, by the trapezius muscle, which takes its origin from the occipital protuberance and ridge and spinous processes of the cervical and dorsal vertebræ, and is inserted into the outer third of the clavicle and into the scapula ; in the latter its insertion can be traced into the inner border of the acromion, and along the inner (upper) border of the spine of the scapula. By its contraction it raises the shoulder, and, when not otherwise prevented, rotates the scapula on an antero-posterior axis so as to bring its upper portion nearer to the spinal column, while the lower angle is turned outwards. It is chiefly the upper portion of the muscle that contracts in this process, the lower portion being only employed in holding the spine of the scapula downwards and inwards.

Fig. 1 shows the muscles of the back of the trunk. The fibres of the trapezius are marked 1 ; 2 denotes the fibres of the deltoid muscle, which are inserted into the outer (lower) edge of the spine of the scapula

opposite those of the trapezius; they can work together with those of the trapezius when the arm is
to be set in motion. If, however, the arm is fixed,
and only the scapula is left free, then their action, as
will be evident, is opposed—*i.e.*, when the fibres of
one muscle contract, those of the other attached to the
scapula opposite them are stretched out. The great

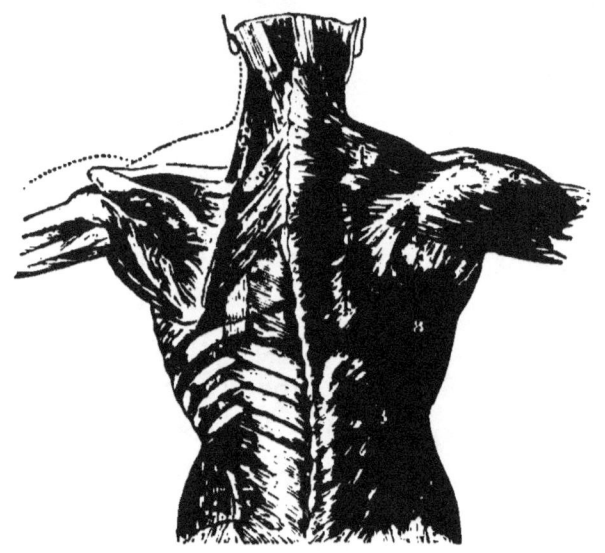

FIG. 1.

flat dorsal muscle (*M. latissimus dorsi*), which also
moves the arm, is marked 3. On the other side
of the trunk the trapezius and latissimus dorsi have
been removed so as to leave the scapula with the
muscles of the arm exposed, as also the muscles
running from the border of the scapula to the
spinal column (5), which raise the scapula and at
the same time bring it nearer to the median line

(*M. rhomboideus*, also called *M. rhomboideus major*
and *minor*, because it is often divided into two un-
equal portions). Lastly, at 6 is shown another muscle,
which runs from the upper and inner corner of the
scapula to the transverse processes of the four upper
cervical vertebræ, and by its contraction raises the
scapula in a more perpendicular direction (*Levator
anguli scapulæ*).

It is evident, therefore, that the contour in question
must depend largely on the action of the arm. When
the arm is moved upwards and outwards, the shoulder
is also raised, and the fibres of the trapezius descending
laterally from the neck must contract, that is, they
all become shorter and thicker, and consequently the
muscle forms under the skin a convex mass of flesh.
When, on the other hand, the arm is moved as if to
reach the hollow of the knee of the other side from
behind, then those same fibres are stretched, *i.e.*, they
become longer and therefore thinner, and the convexity
disappears.

But, apart from changes occasioned by such actions,
we meet with very marked individual variations in
the course taken by this line.

On looking at various figures with the arm hanging
perpendicularly downwards so as completely to relax
the trapezius, we find that some have a distinct convexity between the top of the shoulder and the neck,
as for instance in the Venus de Medicis and in Holbein's
Lais Corinthiaca (Fig. 2), while others have no convexity at all, and the line of the neck passes into that

of the shoulder in a gentle curve, so that when it
reaches the top of the shoulder its direction has
been altered through nearly 90° without exhibiting
a single point of inflection, to use a geometrical
phrase.   An instance is shown in Fig. 3, taken from
the frescoes of Orcagna in Sta. Maria Novella, at
Florence.   Either line may have a good effect, but

FIG. 2.

the latter one is only appropriate to delicate youthful
figures, the former presupposing a riper form and
well-developed muscles.

When fat is present in any quantity, it is always
an important element in the convexity.   It may also
happen that the difference in the two lines is connected
with variations of tone of the trapezius.   Since this
muscle holds the shoulder in readiness for and assists

to bring about every desired movement of the arm, it is seldom completely at rest ; that is to say, even when it gives no external sign of activity, it is receiving from the central nervous system continuous impulses, which maintain the shoulder in the proper position for any change in the position of the arm. These

FIG. 3.

impulses vary in frequency and strength according to the constitution and temperament of the individual. Further, the convexity would seem to be more frequent among people with short necks than with long ones ; though this perhaps is related to the fact that the fibres of the trapezius running from the edge of the shoulder to the upper cervical vertebræ have a shorter and less perpendicular course.

Many persons, who have this convexity in a marked degree, appear to be long-necked without really being so, simply because the shoulder lies unusually low—the reason being that the thorax is not proportionately developed in its upper part, and so causes a depression of the outer end of the clavicle. If, however, the inner extremity of the latter bone is also depressed by reason of the first rib being inclined too much downwards, the neck is actually lengthened, since the fossa of the neck is then situated lower down. The art of the patch-and-powder period offers abundant examples of this type.

Such figures are peculiar in that they appear to have longer necks when seen from in front than from behind. In front the neck is long on account of the low position of the fossa; seen from behind it is shorter, because the cervical vertebræ and their inter-vertebral discs are not abnormally long; and hence the fibres of the trapezius and the subjacent structures in the region of the neck follow the usual track, and are merely carried farther down in their outward course so as to reach the low-lying shoulder.

A defect of the neck occurring not infrequently in many districts consists in its girth being increased from above downwards. The depression bounding the neck at its lower end, and separating it from the sternum, the fossa of the neck—which however is only, strictly speaking, a fossa in lean individuals—has in this instance vanished, and the lower part of the neck seen in front has the appearance of being flat

and wide. A neck of this kind may occur in combination with absolutely flawless beauty in the rest of
the body; but the artist must nevertheless beware of
even attempting to reproduce it, as these necks are
found most frequently in regions where wens and
goitres are prevalent, and constitute, in fact, the commencement of these pathological deformities. In these
and other forms of neck we find the contour in profile
divided from the line of the lower jaw by a sharp
receding angle. This is eminently unpleasing, and
even in ancient times sculptors selected attitudes in
which the neck was slightly bent at the nape, while
the head was turned upwards, so as to give a better
line to the contour when seen in profile. Naturally,
it depends on the nature of the model what can be
accomplished in this respect in dealing with the living
subject. There are, however, models to be found who,
in an appropriate position, leave nothing to be desired
with regard to this line.

In the male, especially in heroic figures, prominence
of the two sterno-mastoid muscles (*Mm. sterno-cleido-
mastoidei*) may be an ornament, but in the female it
is ugly; and many a woman's figure, distinguished
by a well-developed muscular system, is marred by it.
Some figures, however, with well-developed muscles
are free from this defect, because the parts surrounding
the muscles in question are well provided with fat.
But a further factor comes into play—viz., whether
the muscles are favourably placed as regards their
points of insertion. It is favourable when the skull

has a small base, so that the two muscles lie not too far apart, and when the upper end of the sternum and the inner extremities of the clavicles adjoining are not over-prominent.

Besides, the artist can do much in determining his choice of attitude. The most favourable is that above mentioned, in which the neck is somewhat inclined forward at the nape and the head is slightly raised, the face looking to the front or a little to one side. The sterno-mastoid muscles should be neither contracted nor stretched out, but relaxed, so that they may accommodate themselves to the surrounding soft parts and avoid any constriction of the skin.

In the choice of a female model the rule holds good that the neck is to be preferred which, in different aspects, offers somewhat concave and gently-curved contours. If the anterior outline in profile view is straight, it will make an ugly angle with the lower jaw, while convexity of the same line implies either a faulty structure of the cervical region of the spinal column, or a swelling in the region of the thyroid body. Convexity of the anterior line in three-quarter view is the effect either of masculine development of the sterno-mastoid muscles or of swollen veins in the neck. Convexity of the lateral contours of the neck, when seen from in front, may arise from a swelling of the thyroid body, or else from excessive development of the sterno-mastoid muscles.

We now approach the question whether a long neck, a so-called swan's neck, is beautiful or not. Among the ancients the neck, save in a few Tanagra statuettes is not long; it has the proportions of the average necks we see every day around us. A preference for long slender necks shows itself first in the later middle ages and early renaissance, and is associated with a preference for slender forms in general. Thus the neck in the Venus of Sandro Botticelli is in keeping with the character of the whole figure—she could have no other; but whether one ought to be roused to enthusiasm over such a figure, as many people have been in recent times, is a matter of individual taste. As I shall often have occasion to refer to this figure, I have reproduced it here (Fig. 4).*

A long neck joined to a body that is neither tall nor slender produces a disagreeable effect. Length of neck is naturally related to the length of the spinal column, and therefore of the trunk. Accordingly, if the neck is too long in relation to the entire length of the body, and, given a certain height of the whole figure, the portion above the pubes is longer than the portion below it, it follows that the legs must be too short. During the German renaissance, and also,

---

* Though I am not one of those who worship this figure, I am by no means insensible to the poetry and delicacy with which the whole composition is penetrated, or to the dewy freshness which pervades the picture. But, however much we may feel ourselves prepossessed in favour of the genial and original artist from whose school Filippino Lippi emanated, we must not blind ourselves to defects when we are considering individual figures by themselves, and comparing their structural details with the antique.

though less frequently, in the late Italian renaissance, forms are met with which offend in this respect.

Finally, I must repeat that the lower the shoulders are placed the longer does the neck appear to be. The position of the shoulders in turn depends upon that of the clavicles, and this again on the structure of the thorax, so that with a thorax normally developed in a strong and healthy subject abnormally low shoulders are not readily found.

Thus a long neck, although, when it is cylindrical and flexible, in a good spiral line, it may exhibit a feeling of considerable elegance, can only be accounted beautiful if justified by its association with the rest of the figure.

The position of the shoulders is liable to change in one and the same individual, inasmuch as the thorax, while expanding in inspiration, lifts up the shoulder girdle which rests upon it (*cf.* Langer, *loc. cit.*, p. 189). It is well known that fright and surprise are accompanied by a sudden inspiration, not, however, immediately followed by an expiration. Under such circumstances one of the means of characterisation is to place the shoulders slightly higher than they naturally would be in the same figure in a condition of complete repose.

On the female neck may often be seen one or two lines encircling it. They are not folds, though they are the traces of folds which were present during childhood. They were observed and reproduced by the sculptors of antiquity, and may be seen in

FIG 4.

several figures of Venus. When they are met with in the living model they should be carefully copied, for they are an ornament to the female model, inasmuch as they indicate a normal and healthy development in youth, and generally occur only on a fresh skin and one well-knit to the subjacent structures. They must not be confounded with folds such as are easily formed on a slack skin in movements of the neck. C. Rochet remarks : " The folds on the anterior part of the neck are never marks of age and ugliness ; on the contrary, they are found to the number of one or two in young and comely persons only, provided that they are not too thin. It is otherwise with folds on the side of the neck, which are true wrinkles, and make their appearance with age " (" Traité d'Anatomie," p. 210). This statement is so far inaccurate that it lays too much stress on the position of the folds. The main point is rather the nature of the lines, which in the one case are wrinkles, in the other are fine grooves representing vestigial remains of the fat folds in the child's neck. Sometimes they are carried round to the side of the neck, but they are distinguished at a glance by the fact that they are not true folds. The skin is everywhere closely applied to the subjacent structures, and only forms a minute shallow groove along these lines.

Two very ugly pendent longitudinal folds, running from the lower jaw on each side of the chin in a downward direction, are characteristic of old age. They were known to the artists of the later renaissance, and often made use of by them in figures of Furies, impersonations of Plague, etc.

If the finger be passed along the spinous processes of the cervical vertebræ, one such process rather more prominent than the rest will be felt just below the nape, where the neck merges into the back.   This is the so-called prominent vertebra (*Vertebra prominens*). At this point in many women, even when they do not elsewhere show much tendency to fatness, a more or less extensive mass of connective tissue laden with fat is found.   It is not in itself a disfigurement, but, unless the object be to depict a matronly figure, painters and sculptors should beware of indicating it as it is invariably a sign of advancing years.

II

THE ARM AND HAND.

NEXT to a disproportionate length of the arm, the commonest defects in the structure of the bony frame are over-extension and an oblique attachment of the fore-arm to the upper arm.

The upper extremity of the ulna projects, in a manner familiar to all, beyond the elbow-joint, and thus constitutes the small arm of a lever to which the extensor muscles of the arm are attached. By reason of the very shortness of the arm of the lever on which these muscles work, they are enabled to extend the fore-arm with a rapid motion and drive the fist forward for the purpose of giving a blow or a push. When the arm is bent, this piece of bone forms a projection which has given to the whole bone its German name, *Ellenbogenbein.* If the arm is extended, the side of this bony process, which is turned towards the humerus, fits into a fossa in the latter just above the joint, and thus, by a collision of the two bones, any further extension of the arm is checked.

This does not happen till the fore-arm and upper arm form a straight line, or even, when the extension is carried so far, till the fore-arm forms with the upper arm an obtuse angle on the dorsal side, *i.e.*, that on which the extensor muscles lie. This latter condition is what I term over-extension. I do not care if it be asserted that a certain amount of over-extension is normal. It is true that if we measure, in a large number of individuals, the angle formed on the extensor surface by the bones of the upper and fore-arm when fully extended, we shall not find 180° to be the average, but a slightly smaller angle, because the by no means rare cases of considerable over-extension affect the mean. But such a mean is of doubtful value to the anatomist, and does not concern the artist at all. The latter has to ask himself what is the most beautiful among forms actually coming under observation, and over-extension is unquestionably the reverse of beautiful. I can call to mind an admirable tragic actor who had a majestic figure; it served excellently to display the harmonious plasticity of his movements; but whenever he extended his arm in a moment of passion, the figure was marred by over-extension of the arm.

This feature is peculiarly disagreeable in men of a powerful build. It is more tolerable when present to a slight degree in children and young girls, not as improving the lines, but as helping to characterise the flexibility of the youthful body, and therefore occasionally to be sought after.

The second and very common defect is an oblique attachment of the fore-arm. We must first distinguish between two different positions of the outstretched arm : that in which the thumb lies on the outer side, called supination, and that in which it lies on the inner side, known as pronation. Anatomically the distinction between the two consists in this : that in supination the two bones of the fore-arm, the radius and ulna, lie parallel to one another, whereas in pronation the radius crosses the ulna in an oblique direction. If the arm is flexed at the elbow, and the latter is held close to the body, it will be found that the back of the hand can be turned first upwards and then downwards. Here the angle traversed between pronation and supination extends to about 180°. With the arm extended the hand can be rotated through 270° ; but the additional 90° should not be put down to the account of pronation and supination, but to that of a rotation of the humerus in the shoulder-joint.

After these preliminaries let us consider the out-stretched arm first in supination. If we imagine a straight line drawn through the axis of the upper arm and produced beyond it, such a line will not coincide with the axis of the fore-arm, but will make an angle with it, deviating towards the side of the little finger. Thus, in a sense, every fore-arm is attached obliquely to the upper arm and forms an angle with it.

When, however, we consider the arm in pronation, the case is altered. In order to pass from supination to pronation, we rotate the lower flattened end of the radius round the lower end of the ulna, and the hand revolves on the axis of the little finger, as it were, so that the thumb, which before lay on the outside, comes to lie on the inside. In the process the fore-arm and hand are brought much more nearly into a line with the axis of the upper arm than in supination, because, though the ulna makes the same angle as before with the axial line of the upper arm, yet the whole mass, which formerly lay on the outside of the ulna, is now, so far as it consists of the hand and lower portion of the fore-arm, situated on its inside. The angle formed by the attachment of the ulna to the humerus varies in different people, and is very often too small—smaller, that is, than is consistent with beauty of line; and this is what I mean by an oblique attachment of the fore-arm.

A glance at such an arm when it is extended in supination shows this deformity from the front as well as from behind; but it becomes more marked if that part of the head of the humerus, which is most prominent in front,* be found, and a string be fixed there and stretched thence to the hand, so as to lie between the two tendons of the flexor muscles which project on the fore-arm, close to the wrist, when the hand is flexed towards the fore-arm by muscular contraction and the flexion is prevented by external resistance. These are the tendons of the *M. palmaris*

* This is the so-called lesser tuberosity (*Tuberculum minus*) of the head of the humerus, which lies immediately to the inside and in front of the groove in which the tendon of the long head of the biceps runs up to the shoulder-joint.

longus and of the *M. flexor carpi radialis*, also known as the *radialis internus*. The tightly-stretched string should now pursue the following course :—On the flexor side of the arm, when the hand is in supination, a shallow depression is seen near the elbow. It is caused by the tendon of the great flexor of the arm, the biceps, sinking deep down between the masses of muscle lying on either side of it towards its insertion into the radius. The string should run midway over this depression, or, at any rate, just to one side of the deepest part of it ; and the further the string lies to one side of the median line, the more oblique is the attachment of the fore-arm. I would by no means venture to maintain that a rectilinear attachment of the fore-arm is the most frequent, and therefore normal, in the anthropological sense ; but it is that which may be employed in the most varied attitudes without giving disagreeable lines, and which I therefore must perforce regard as the best for artistic purposes.

An oblique attachment of the fore-arm appears to be more common among women than among men (just as an inward projection of the knee, the so-called knock-kneed condition, is commoner among women) ; at any rate, it is more often remarked in them. Fashionable dress leads them to carry the arm more ·turned outwards than is the case of men. In consequence, the outer condyle of the humerus, which faces to the front in men in a state of repose, is in women turned more outwards, and the inner condyle

more inwards. Thus the common plane of the axis
of the humerus and the axis of rotation of the elbow-
joint would turn one surface to the front and the
other backwards; and this is also the plane in which
the deflection of the obliquely-attached fore-arm falls.
When, therefore, fashionably-dressed and tightly-laced
ladies in whom the fore-arm is obliquely attached are
seen from in front or behind, the defect is observable
in the oblique position of the fore-arm as compared
with the vertically-pendent position of the upper arm,
in spite of the loosely-hanging hands being usually
pronated.

C. Langer has remarked (*loc. cit.*, p. 269) that the
ulna, when flexed on the humerus, does not lie
directly over it, but is deflected to the inside. This
deflection becomes marked in proportion to the
obliquity of the attachment of the fore-arm, since
the axis of rotation is proportionately deflected from
the position at right angles to the longitudinal axis
of the humerus. Just as the knock-kneed condition
has its origin in a deformity of the lower end of the
femur, so the obliquely-attached fore-arm arises from
a deformity of the lower extremity of the humerus,
and not from any deformity of the ulna.

Every one can lay the tips of the fingers on the
shoulder-joint of the same side, but the arm and hand
do not take up a similar position in the process in
every case. The more obliquely the fore-arm is
attached to the arm, the more must the hand be
turned outwards, or else the humerus must be propor-

tionately rotated outwards. This is readily explained by the difference of position which the strongly-flexed fore-arm assumes with regard to the upper arm, according as its attachment is straight or oblique.

Nevertheless, an accurate knowledge of the shape of the arm is requisite to enable the observer, on looking at an arm even when strongly flexed, as *e.g.* in the Sleeping Ariadne or the so-called Diana of Gabii, to determine at once whether it is obliquely attached or not. When, therefore, the artist has to work closely on the lines of his model, and the latter is defective in this particular, he should endeavour to conceal the defect by means of an appropriate attitude, having recourse either to flexion or to pronation. Seeing that the oblique fore-arm is deflected outwards from the axis of the humerus in the extended position, and inwards when completely flexed, there is always a median position which shows the form of the arm to the best advantage. But how obliquity of the fore-arm, even when moderately bent and in pronation, will yet betray itself, may be seen in Fig. 5, which is reproduced from a photograph from life.

On the other hand the defect may, as we have said, be concealed by careful arrangement. A favourite attitude with sculptors is that of a girl plaiting her hair. In this instance the artist may copy his model faithfully, even when the fore-arm is not faultless, if only the inner condyle of the humerus does not make an angular projection. One thing, however, must be guarded against : the hand belonging to the side on which the plait hangs down should be the lower one, that of the opposite side the upper ; by this means a degree of flexion is obtained in both arms, such as to prevent the defect being perceptible. In this way arms may be available, which would be of no

FIG. 5.

use when extended in supination. Very slight defects of this nature may become imperceptible in the extended arm, as soon as it is pronated. It may be formulated as a rule that this has taken place if the axis of the outstretched pronated arm appears straight.

How much pronation helps the appearance of a moderately oblique fore-arm is evident from Fig. 6,

which is a reduced copy of a drawing by G. L. Rochet
(from C. Rochet, " Traité d'Anatomic," Fig. 28).   I
have indicated by a dotted line the direction of the
axis of the upper arm when produced.   It will be seen
that the whole of the carpus lies outside the dotted

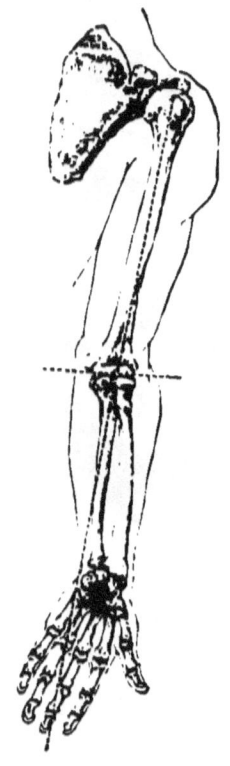

Fig. 6.

line.   In pronation the lower end of the radius is
rotated over the ulna, so that the former comes to
lie on the inside of the lower extremity of the latter,
and then the produced axis of the upper arm will
pass through the carpus.

I have also indicated the axis of rotation of the

elbow-joint. In this it will become clear why, when the arm is strongly flexed, the wrist comes to lie more and more inside the shoulder, in proportion to the degree of obliquity of the fore-arm. It would lie directly on the shoulder if the axis of rotation stood exactly at right angles to the axis of the humerus, or, what comes to the same thing, if the plane in which the fore-arm moves during flexion were parallel to the axis of the humerus. This is not the case, however. The external superior angle formed by the axis of rotation with that of the humerus is an acute angle, and consequently the wrist, which, when the arm was extended in supination, was deflected outwards, will be deflected inwards when flexed through more than 90°.

Hitherto I have distinguished between the axis of the upper arm and that of the humerus. By the former I do not mean the axis of the bone, nor the axis round which the pendent upper arm rotates in the shoulder-joint, for the latter axis would pass through a point the horizontal distance of which from the surface of the joint is not altered during the rotation. What is meant is the straight line drawn through the mean centre of a continuous series of transverse sections of the upper arm. This is the line which the eye seeks, for it would be the true geometrical axis of the upper arm if the latter had the form of a cylinder. If produced, it must still pass through the middle of the carpus, if in pronation the outstretched arm is to appear straight.

A peculiarly unpleasing effect is wrought by the combination of obliquity of the fore-arm with over-extension. When such an arm is extended in supination, the inner prominence of the lower extremity of the humerus makes an angular projection on the inner side, and yields a very ugly line.

I have shown above how the lines of the extended fore-arm with only moderate obliquity of attachment may be improved by pronation. If, however, the angle resulting from the obliquity is still further removed from 180°, the lines will continue to be bad in pronation. The angular prominence formed by the inner condyle of the humerus is then no longer masked by pronation, but is, in fact, rendered more emphatic by the depression which is formed some three finger-breadths below it, and which arises from the state of tension in which the fascia of the fore-arm is maintained by its connection with the tendon of the biceps ; another depression lies opposite it on the radial side of the arm. Since the arm in being pronated is, as a rule, also rotated in the shoulder-joint, the angle between the humerus and ulna, which with the arm extended in supination faced outwards, now faces to the front, whereby the lower extremity of the ulna becomes prominent as compared with the upper extremity. The radius is now rotated over the ulna thus obliquely placed, and, when pronation is complete, in such a way that its anterior end lies behind, or, if the arm is raised, below that of the ulna. All these concomitants yield restless and inharmonious lines, which have a bad effect æsthetically in the male and female figure alike.

The form of the male upper arm depends so much on the muscular development and the action represented, that further details would be out of place here. In the female it is generally accounted beautiful in proportion to its roundness when the fore-arm is partly flexed ; among the ancients, too, the upper arm gravitates towards a cylindrical form. In the renaissance period, however, we frequently find examples of an upper arm which, as is often the case in nature, is laterally compressed ; and the contrast is heightened between the more powerful development in the direction of depth, *i.e.*, in an antero-posterior direction of the upper arm, and that of the fore-arm in the direction of breadth. The masters of the renaissance were, in fact, more rigidly naturalist than is usually admitted in current statements on the subject.

A cylindrical upper arm is materially dependent on the following conditions : viz., that the olecranon be short and project but little during flexion of the arm ; that the tendon of the biceps be short and be inserted as high up as possible into the radius ; and that the subcutaneous fat be well-developed in relation to the muscles. Boys, as a rule, have flatter arms than girls. Whereas the later masters usually gave female arms to their angels, even when otherwise of a male type, Andrea del Sarto by preference furnished his with boys' arms.

Very marked and beautiful girls' arms were given

by Palma Giovane to his angels, in whom, however, the female type prevails throughout.

The effect of the muscle tone must also be considered in connection with the form of the arm. Living muscle is so soft when relaxed that every portion of it obeys the law of gravity. It is softer even than at any time after death, when once *rigor mortis* has set in, although when the rigor is at an end it may seem as if complete flexibility of the limbs were restored.

Nevertheless, in different individuals differences in the resisting power of the relaxed muscles are perceptible to the touch. This is generally attributed to so-called muscular tone. I will not enter here into the various views which are held as to its origin, but will content myself with mentioning its existence and that of the differences above referred to, and will only add that the latter have nothing to do with bodily strength. Some men possess great bodily strength though their muscles are excessively soft when relaxed, and offer very little resistance to the touch. But the softer the relaxed muscles are, the less will they tend to retain their natural shape, and so adapt themselves to the cylindrical form which the skin and fat layer stretched over them seek to give them.

This softness of the relaxed muscles is connected with another appearance which deserves mention here.

If the pronated fore-arm be flexed to rather less than a right angle, and so supported that the upper arm forms a horizontal bridge between the shoulder-joint and the support, the biceps becomes relaxed, and owing to its weight the middle part, being but slightly bound to the surrounding tissues, sinks down until the entire muscle acquires a bow shape, convex below and concave above. This gives to the anterior lower side of the upper arm an outline which at the first glance is repellent, because we are not accustomed to see the line in this shape. However, this line, which can easily be demonstrated on any model, should not remain unnoticed. Figures not infrequently occur with the pronated fore-arm flexed and supported, and in these the appearance above mentioned must be indicated in order to express completely the condition of repose which, as a rule, they exhibit.

Although the ancients gave their preference to a cylindrical arm in the female, and that shape is in reality highly esteemed, yet it cannot be denied that with regard to the lines it presents it fails under some circumstances to be so attractive as a form which is less nearly cylindrical.

A female arm in which, owing to a strongly developed muscular system, the triangular muscle of the shoulder (*M. deltoideus*) is well marked, and, further, the extensors and flexors can be distinguished in their respective positions, more or less, according to the action of the arm, may be beautiful and excellently adapted for reproduction in the arts. Such an arm will not have a masculine appearance, provided that the bones are cast in a feminine mould, and that the furrows between the muscles are not too much emphasized. This will be secured if a moderate layer of fat fills up the hollows, so that they pass gradually into the elevations. This form of arm is specially suited for figures of caryatides, but even the greatest masters have not hesitated to give it to other female figures. For instance, it occurs in the just-created Eve of Michelangelo on the ceiling of the Sistine Chapel, and in Raffaelle's figure of Peace in the Vatican. A less strongly marked but instructive arm of this type, modelled with very little aid from extraneous sources, is found in a figure holding a trumpet and standard by Perino del Vaga, which hangs near the principal door of the long hall in the Doria Palace at Genoa.

This form of upper arm, which by means of its defined muscular system makes itself intelligible to the mind, has the further advantage for the sculptor of presenting a greater variety of line from different points of view. Its successful presentation is no easy matter, and demands a good model and careful insistence on detail. Quite recently Agostino Felici, of Venice, has given a brilliant proof of the superiority of this type in his Veneziana (Local Exhibition in the Palazzo Pisani in the autumn of 1881). The problem here was the more difficult as the arm was a fat one. Notwithstanding, the forms of the structures lying under the surface were distinctly recognisable.

It will be well to notice here a prejudice which is widely spread among the public. Many mothers are afraid of their daughters doing any exercises with the arms, lest the latter should acquire a masculine shape. It is remarkable, however, that no apprehension is shown if these same daughters practise the piano for several hours every day, exerting certain muscles of the fore-arm in a violent and exclusive fashion in doing so. Yet there is, in general, no foundation for the fear. Bodily exercises only affect the form of the body disadvantageously under two conditions: either when they are begun at too early an age, or else when they are so excessive as to produce emacia- tion. That violent exercise may be taken without injury in this respect is proved by the well-known gymnast who, under the name of Leona Dare,* has displayed the beauty of her arms in all the great cities of the world.

A well-rounded upper arm is as rare among youthful members of the higher and middle classes as it is common among women who are in the second summer of their beauty. Formerly this was even more striking than at the present day, when in many girls the arms are better developed by exercises.

Thinness of the upper arm must not, however, be attributed solely to want of muscular development, but also to absence of fat. In a healthy person, leading an easy life, fat is chiefly deposited in the tissues through middle life, generally from the twenty-fifth, and not infrequently from the twentieth year onwards. However, this deposit of fat takes place

* The Leona Dare here referred to was, in the seventies, a member of Renz's Circus at Vienna.

especially in certain regions, while in others a decrease may be simultaneously observed. It may be said that the fat migrates at different periods of life from one part of the body to another; and to this fact is related the frequency with which, in young girls, the upper arm is so thin as to be positively ugly. The phenomenon is so familiar that no intelligent sculptor would model the upper arm of a Hebe so as to be thick in comparison with the fore-arm.

There is yet another defect of beauty which occurs in both sexes, and is also reproduced occasionally in sculpture. Sometimes we receive an impression as if the upper arm did not run truly up to the shoulder, and did not fit on to the joint, but rather to a point slightly lower down, near the armpit. I was first struck by this in a St. Sebastian. At first I thought it was merely a piece of bad drawing; but afterwards I was convinced that the fault really lay with the model.

If the bone of the humerus be looked at straight from in front or from behind, and an imaginary median or axial line be drawn through the lower third of it, and if a similar axial line be then drawn through the upper portion of the bone, it will be found that the two axes do not form exactly a straight line, but make an angle, an extremely obtuse one indeed, but still an angle. This change in the direction of the bone commences in the lower half of its middle third part. It is still visible when the bone is turned round until its dorsal surface (*i.e.* that which looks behind when the arm is rotated outwards) is turned outwards, somewhat as it is when the arm is placed akimbo, only the change of direction is now seen to commence at a slightly different spot. It is this deflection in the shaft of the humerus—a deflection varying in amount in different individuals—which gives rise to the above-mentioned defect. It is greatly intensified by leanness, that is, by absence of fat, in a well-developed muscular system. This causes the deceptive appearance of the arm not fitting into the joint, when the shape of the bone is defective, to be very striking, by reason of the depres sion which lies between the insertion of the deltoid and the origin of the great extensor muscle of the arm, and by reason of the shape given to the dorsal surface of the upper arm by the fleshy belly of that muscle when the muscles on the flexor side are similarly developed.

Besides lack of fat, it is mainly the length of the olecranon (pointed elbow) that contributes to the deceptive appearance when the arm is bent at a right angle, because the insertion of the great extensor tendon is set far back, and its spreading out gives rise to a flat surface that yields no line with the contours of the flexor side to lead the eye directly to the centre of the ball-and-socket joint forming the shoulder. When, therefore, a figure has to be represented as holding the arm akimbo, or as lifting or holding an object with the arm bent at a right angle, it is necessary to examine the model well to see whether his arm is suitable for the

given action, or whether it should be replaced by
another.   But in this case the defect we are considering, besides its practical interest, has this theoretical quality, that we know the reason why we feel
the lines to be bad : we feel them to be bad because
they do not guide us to a spontaneous, conception of
the true connection of the limbs.

The form of the fore-arm in the male, as in the
case of the upper arm, is so much determined by
the development and action of the muscles as to
allow of no special remark as to the upper part of it,
at any rate.   In the female its beauty is held to consist in its approach to a cylindrical form in its upper
portion when bent towards the upper arm.   If a
transverse section be taken in imagination through
the fore-arm so bent, such a section will approximate
most nearly among familiar geometrical figures to an
ellipse whose major axis runs obliquely from above
and outwards in a downward and inward direction.
In pronation its direction will tend to be more
vertical, in supination more horizontal.   Now, a
woman's arm is considered more beautiful in proportion as the excentricity of the ellipse is diminished,
i.e., the more it approximates to a circle.   Of course
it does not follow that the artist should make the arm
cylindrical, but only that he should prefer that model
in whom the flexed fore-arm is round to one in whom
it is flattened.   The extended fore-arm is always
more or less flat, especially in supination; less so in
pronation.

In figures of Hercules the lower portion of the fore-arm is often invested with an unusual breadth. This can only be caused by the large space occupied by the extremity of the radius, which is flat and broad beneath, and that of the ulna, which lies beside the former. It is, therefore, breadth and massiveness of bone that are here represented. This may be appropriate to Hercules, who is more or less a personification of brute force; otherwise one is inclined to maintain that a man's strength lies in his muscles rather than in his bones, and it would be extremely inappropriate to characterise by such means the supernatural strength of an Achilles.

The lower part of the fore-arm should not be made too broad in the female, and its diameter, measured from the dorsal to the under side, should not be too much reduced in proportion to the transverse diameter. Fore-arms marred by this defect are found especially among the German races and in individuals of bony build. German sculptors are easily misled into reproducing them by their native models. Some fore-arms, nevertheless, are to be found that have a broad lower extremity, and yet are not without a beauty of their own. Here, however, it is not the breadth of the bones that determines the form, but a layer of fat which is developed much more than usual on the outer side of both radius and ulna. It is present in arms that are furnished generally with a considerable amount of adipose tissue. Such arms usually terminate towards the wrist in a slight depression, which gives them a certain resemblance to children's arms. This type of arm was most frequently adopted by masters of the period of the Decadence, but it also occurs in the work of Titian and Correggio. A certain breadth is desirable in the lower portion of the fore-arm when the hand either is not small or is broadened out by action, as, for instance, in grasping a staff; for if the line of transition from the arm to the hand expands too suddenly, it produces a bad effect, and one to be avoided if possible.

Sometimes a shallow furrow runs transversely across the lower surface of the fore-arm. It lies at a distance below the elbow about equal to the breadth of the ring and little fingers put together. In appearance it resembles the lines on the neck which I have described above as children's lines. Artists have seldom taken any notice of it; but when present in the model it may be rendered without demur, though, of course, without exaggeration. Like the lines on the neck, it has nothing to do with wrinkles or folds, and may be present on a perfectly fresh and youthful skin.

The lower surface of the lower portion of the fore-arm also deserves special attention. On it may be seen in youthful individuals of both sexes, when not too lean, two shallow furrows when the hand is bent backwards as if to rest the head on it. One lies near the median line, but a little on the side towards the thumb. It follows the inner border of the tendon of the *flexor carpi radialis*. The other one lies more to the side of the little finger, and follows the line of the tendon of the *flexor carpi ulnaris.* Between the two, when the hand is bent in the position above described, lies an elevation, which, as it is continued upwards, is merged in the general rounded under surface of the arm. It is caused by the bent-back carpus thrusting forwards the soft parts lying on its lower surface. When the hand is straightened and then flexed, the appearance of the parts is changed ; and if the hand be passively flexed, the median elevation may be made to sink in so far as to be converted into a shallow depression. It is quite permissible for the artist to reproduce these phenomena if he meets with them in a well-shaped and not over-lean arm ; but he should guard against one thing—viz., representing the tightly-stretched tendons. They are always ugly, and it is justifiable to indicate them only when the subject demands the presentation of violently-contracted muscles.

I ought also to mention a particular deformity to which the fore-arm is subject when it is flexed and also weighted, especially in persons who are lean, and whose muscles are not well developed.

From the lower third of the humerus there arises from the external condyloid ridge a powerful muscle called the supinator longus ; it runs down the fore-arm, passing about halfway down into its tendon, and is inserted by means of the latter into the lower end of the radius, along the .base of the so-called styloid process, and therefore on the thumb side of the radius. The chief function of this muscle consists, as its name implies, in bringing about supination. When the fore-arm is held in the elbow-joint firmly in any position by means of the flexors and extensors, and then pronated, the origin and insertion of the supinator longus are thereby shifted away from each other; if it is now contracted, it tends to bring these two points into their original positions, and so restores the condition of supination.

Besides this main function it has also a subsidiary function. When the arm is flexed, and radius and ulna are held firmly in their parallel position by other muscles, the points of origin and insertion of the supinator longus are so placed that its contraction causes a further flexion of the arm. It may thus serve to flex the arm or keep it flexed, in accordance with the principle that all the muscles of the human body that are able to support one another do so.

If the arms are bent and weighted—for instance by a heavy vessel held in the hands before one—the contracted supinator longus projects as a ridge on the upper part of the fore-arm extending to the upper arm. The lines of the arms, especially when not well provided with fat, may be very much disfigured by this action. This disfigurement is also exhibited in individuals with undeveloped muscles, as in that case the muscle does not become prominent by its swelling up, but by its being seen to be tightly stretched between two fixed points. Indeed, if a fat layer is absent in addition, the disfigurement becomes even more marked than in muscular persons, since the muscle is flatter and more angular. Further, this action may render the tendon of the biceps, and even the portion of it which joins the fascia of the fore-arm, disagreeably conspicuous.

A very common defect in models of German origin is the excessive prominence of the lower extremity of the ulna behind the wrist. I merely mention this for completeness' sake, as the defect itself is so ugly that no artist would think of reproducing it on any female arm which was intended to be beautiful. Sometimes, however, this does happen in mediæval pictures, in consequence of lean and bony models having been selected. Nor less ugly is the pointed projection of the upper extremity of the ulna in the flexed arm, the "pointed elbow," which is the result of unusual length of the olecranon, and of leanness. This, too, has not always been avoided by artists ; and, among other instances, it is a blemish in the Venus of Sandro Botticelli (cf. Fig. 4, on p. 31).

A long olecranon is, under any circumstances, a defect. If the arm is bent at an angle of less than 90°, it makes a pointed elbow ; if at right angles, the contour of the extensor surface of the upper arm is spoilt, because it then descends in a straight line, and forms a right angle with the contour of the extensor surface of the fore-arm, whereas with a short olecranon it is curved at the lower end, so as to form a rounded obtuse angle instead of a right angle.

Finally, if the arm is extended, a long olecranon in this position reaches so far upwards that it pushes the tendon of insertion of the triceps, and partially also the skin before it, and so forms an ugly fold, which, if a considerable amount of fat be present, yields a very prominent and vulgar-looking outline. A short olecranon in the same position gives rise to a small fossa only, which may be more or less deep according as over-extension is present or not.

It should be added that not only the length of the olecranon, but also its shape, is a matter of consideration. When the posterior edge of the ulna runs up in a concave curve to the end of the olecranon and forms a sharp angle with its terminal surface, the elbow is more pointed than when the bone is more rounded at its termination. An example of an elbow that is beautiful in spite of strong flexion is afforded by the so-called Diana of Gabii.*

A long olecranon generally occurs as part of a fore-arm that is itself unusually long; and this is oftener the case in long-armed than in short-armed individuals. And thus a pointed elbow is more frequent among the former. The upper arm may also, however, be too long, not merely in comparison with the length of the body and with the length of

* I follow the usual custom in giving it this name, though, with C. Friederichs ("Bausteine zur Geschichte der griechisch-römischen Plastik," I. The Casts in the New Museum at Berlin), I cannot see in this admirable figure anything but a girl in a short chiton, about to put on or take off her upper garment.

the trunk from the scalp to the pubes, but also in comparison with the fore-arm, though this would seem not often to be the case.

Long arms are notoriously ugly, and are an attribute of the lower races. A model is not easy to find in whom the arms are too short as compared with the legs, but there is no lack of specimens in whom they are too long.

Apart, however, from the length and shape of the olecranon, another feature has to be considered as affecting the beauty of the elbow.

If a longitudinal axis be imagined drawn through the humerus, the middle portion of which must for the present be regarded as being cylindrical, this axis will not cut the axis of rotation of the elbow-joint, but will pass behind it on the extensor side. This is connected with the fact that the lower third of the humerus is slightly bent forward towards the flexor side. By this means the prominence of the olecranon is diminished. When, therefore, the arm is bent at a right angle, unless the olecranon is of excessive length, the angle formed at the elbow by the ulnar outline of the fore-arm and the outline of the upper arm is not a right angle, but an obtuse angle, which, as we have seen, has an agreeable effect.

The above-mentioned bend in the humerus is very rarely too much accentuated in men who otherwise have well-shaped limbs, but it frequently happens that it is not marked enough, particularly among the German races ; the result being that the form of the flexed arm is angular, even when the length of the olecranon alone is not sufficient to account for this. The defect becomes especially prominent when the extensor muscles of the upper arm are poorly developed, and but little fat lies between them and the skin.

Lastly, I must mention the inner condyle of the humerus, which, though it has no bearing upon the shape of the elbow in the strict sense of the word, can yet give the whole joint an ugly angular appearance by jutting out too much, or by carrying its sharp edge too far backwards.

In passing on to the consideration of the hand we are met, first, by the mode in which the wrist is connected with the middle portion of the hand or metacarpus. Here we find two types prevailing. According to one, the wrist (by which I do not mean the bones of the carpus, but the entire section of the limb corresponding to the carpus) is so attached to the hand, that both lie in the same plane when the hand is pronated and extended in a line with the arm ; according to the other, the wrist makes with the hand an obtuse angle at the dorsal surface. The latter form is the more beautiful, as it gives a far more graceful line to the hand when extended in pronation.

If the eye follow the dorsal contour of the fore-arm in an example of the first type, it will be seen to run straight without any break into that of the back of the hand. In the second type, however, it forms an arched elevation over the wrist, and only regains a course parallel to its former one at the commencement of the hand. In this instance the wrist is recognised as a distinct piece intervening between fore-arm and hand, whereas in the first type nothing is distinguishable between arm and hand but a mere border-line.

Likewise in flexion of the hand on the fore-arm

FIG. 7.

the contour yielded by the second type has more movement and variety, as it is, in addition, more advantageous, when the hand is bent backwards, because it offers a more rounded and less angular curve. As an example, I give in the accompanying woodcut (Fig. 7) the clasped hands of Domenichino's Magdalen in the Pitti Gallery. Since the second type is rarer in the Northern than in the Latin races, the artist should be on his guard against reproducing anything distinctly ungraceful in his Northern model.

The hand is a part of the body constantly exposed to view. Its effect is always wrought through its form alone, and not through psychical elements, as in the case of the face. Perhaps this is the reason why there is so much unanimity in the judgments expressed about it. If one does occasionally meet with an unreasoning enthusiasm for exceptionally small or unusually long and narrow hands, it should be regarded merely as the affectation of a few lay persons, in no degree affecting the general verdict. To one or two points I must refer in detail.

In hands that are in general well-made but not fat, the fingers taper regularly from the base to the tip, neither becoming thicker at the joints than between them, nor the reverse to any considerable extent. And this is the form given them in art. Fingers which are thicker at the joints are so obviously ugly that they are now never reproduced. It was done sometimes in the middle ages and in the period of transition to the renaissance, at a time when the figure of the Madonna was still endowed with the leanness of asceticism. The latest example of this that occurs to me came from the brush of Fra Filippo Lippi, and is the Madonna, No. 162, in the Corsini Gallery at Florence. No master, perhaps, has been so misinterpreted in regard to his artistic intentions as Fra Filippo.

Female hands do, however, occur in which the

fingers taper very markedly, though irregularly, from root to tip. In these the first phalanx of the finger, reckoning from its base, has a more or less developed dorsal cushion of connective tissue and fat, giving rise to a not inconsiderable thickening. The second phalanx has a similar though smaller cushion; while the third phalanx is narrow and bears narrow nails, which lengthwise are straight, but transversely are cylindrically arched.*

The back of this kind of hand is usually somewhat fat, sufficiently so to make it even and to exclude any prominence of the tendons and blood-vessels. Such hands occur by no means exclusively in fat women, but are likewise met with in quite young girls, mainly in North Italy, and especially in the Venetian territory. They have been introduced only to a very limited extent in monumental art, though not infrequently present in figures of Venus and female figures of a genre character. They offer more mobile, less severe lines than hands in which the fingers taper quite uniformly. This is especially noticeable when the fingers are moderately flexed, and at the same

* This form of nail, which should not be too short as measured from the free border to the fold of skin, is an ornament to the female hand. Nails that are short, broad and flat, or more arched lengthwise than across, are vulgar. Ribera had a peculiar liking for painting vulgar nails; or, rather, his coarse naturalism led him to copy the models he picked up in the streets.

The arching of the nails increases from the index finger to the little finger. The difference is greatest between index and middle finger, least between the ring and little finger.

time bent backwards towards the back of the hand. This bending back of the fingers may be reproduced in art, without hesitation, when appropriate to the subject; for it may be regarded as normal in the female sex, and is not infrequently found in men, though in them it gives an impression of softness and of feminine character. A less marked but normal bending backwards, produced passively by mere pressure on the balls of the fingers, occurs between the middle and terminal phalanges.

With respect to the attachment of the finger to the hand, it should be mentioned that a sharp and clean-cut range of basal connections gives better lines than where the fingers are connected at the base by weblike folds of skin. The outline of the hand, with the fingers extended and separated, should exhibit the intervals between them bounded, not by a pointed arch or an acute angle, but by a transverse line, making, with the diverging outlines of the fingers, a right or a more or less obtuse angle.

I must close this section with a warning : arms and hands of remarkable beauty are often met with in women at an age when the rest of the body is no longer fit for representation in the nude. Sometimes, indeed, the arm only developes its full beauty at a comparatively mature age. Now, the sculptor must not be misled into introducing an arm of this type into a figure representing youthful beauty. The arm of the Clio who is inscribing the name of Cavour on his monument in Milan has excited the admiration

of spectators innumerable; but it is the arm of a
lady who has attained the years of ripe experience, as
indeed befits the muse of history, and not that of a
girlish beauty.

However, instances of the long-continued duration
of a beautifully-formed arm are by no means of
general occurrence among women, even when healthy
and well nourished and developed. Sometimes a
change sets in at quite an early age, which in others
only reveals itself later. It is coincident with a
certain slackness of the skin and also of the muscles
when in a condition of non-activity. Muscles that
are not stimulated to activity, as is well known,
lack firmness of consistency. This quality, as above
mentioned, differs much in individuals, though we are
unable to trace any connection between it and the
degree of muscular power present in any given case.
Slack muscles of this kind are often so soft that,
whenever the surrounding tissues allow of it, they
sink under their own weight and hang down, unless
held up by the tenser surface of a fascia or of the
skin. In consequence, a defect is apt to show itself,
which is observed when the arm is flexed and the
hand pronated. If the arm is well developed, and
also well preserved, it will, under these circumstances,
retain its round shape, not exactly cylindrical, but of
a rounded form, which, in transverse section, becomes
gradually more elliptical towards the wrist. If, however, the arm is not well preserved, but is none the
less well nourished, the line of the ulna will be trace-

5

able on the outside, followed, lower down, by a plane surface, which may even be slightly concave in its upper part, and then by a more or less marked bulging downwards, caused by the slack and pendent pronator and flexor muscles, whereas the extensor surface of the fore-arm, especially in its anterior part, has a flat form.

It is only necessary to open at random the pages of the comic journals to find abundant examples of the characteristic lines of such arms depicted in female humpbacks, washerwomen, etc.; they are, moreover, not absent in the work of Rubens, who dealt with them quite in a serious spirit. At the present day there is little fear of such arms being taken as a pattern; still, the portrait painter should be on his guard, if he meet with them, of giving any indication of such a form. The artist must lend his aid in such a case, and his artistic licence will assuredly be accounted to him for righteousness. It is related of Van Dyck how, on his journey to England, he took with him certain models with remarkably beautiful hands, in order to paint from them the hands in his portraits; and I have never heard that complaint was ever raised against him that the hands in his portraits did not resemble those of the originals.

More conscientious, perhaps, is the course taken by the portrait painter who seeks to display the arm of his sitter to the greatest advantage by selecting an appropriate attitude or action, and also by concealing from view parts that do not gain by being seen.

III

THE BREAST AND SHOULDERS.

THE first point to be considered is the form of the thorax. It should not be flat or at all compressed in front, nor, on the other hand, should the sternum project while the ribs curve round obliquely to join it in front (chicken-breast, *Pectus carinatum*). The more the ribs are arched, the better is the effect. Again, the thorax should not become narrowed in its upper portion too rapidly or too prominently. A broad chest and shoulders—the latter, however, not separated from the former as isolated parts of the structure—are especially favourable to the lines of figures indicative of manly vigour, while the thorax should be of such a compass in its upper part as to bring the breast into direct continuity with the shoulders.

Canova has given us a model of a finely-proportioned thorax in his Perseus. There is a tendency in modern times to depreciate this master, on account of his affectation and the occasional lameness of his composition. But he has a claim to lasting fame, for he was intimately acquainted with the beauties of the human body, of the female body especially, and he

knew how to give them expression.   No one who
goes to Possagno, and studies the collection of casts
from Canova's works preserved there, can fail to
be convinced of this.   I selected his Perseus as an
example because the form of the thorax is there the
leading feature ; the development of the muscles is
comparatively weak.   The ancients conceived their
heroes as more muscular and more powerfully built.

The thorax is always admirably shaped in antique
art, though its dimensions may vary in regard to
capacity, being greatest in the figures of certain gods
and heroes.   Examples of finely-developed muscular
chests are at hand in the sculptures from Pergamon ;
for instance, in the Zeus brandishing the thunderbolt
and the Warrior (Ares ?) who stands opposite Artemis
as she shoots.   The groove over the breast-bone in
many ancient and modern statues corresponds to the
space intervening between the points of origin on
either side of the great pectoral muscle, and is
specially marked in figures of Hercules in order to
emphasize the extraordinary development of those
muscles.

Among the sculptors of the renaissance, who had
not before their eyes daily the athletes of ancient
times, this groove is no longer treated with the same
emphasis.   For instance, in Michelangelo's David it
is altogether absent in the upper, though present in
the lower part.

The defects of most frequent occurrence in the
male thorax are depressions between the breast and

the clavicles, and also between the breast and the shoulders, depressions under the breast, a want of depth in an antero-posterior direction, an uneven sternum, and visibility of the costal cartilages which adjoin it on each side. I shall return to some of these defects in treating of the female thorax, and will now merely add a few remarks on the shoulders in the male.

Every one who has observed the Farnese Hercules closely must have been struck with the apparently unnatural development of the lower portion of the deltoid muscle, and many persons doubtless have attributed it to the same spirit of exaggeration that shows itself in the muscles of the flanks in the same figure. I once, however, observed similar shoulders in a compactly-built gymnast of extraordinary strength. Their shape is due to the rapid convergence and overlapping of the fibres in the lower part of the deltoid, which gives rise to a marked elevation continuous with one a little higher up, which constitutes the lateral curve of the shoulder. In individuals who are very lean and also lack flesh, the head of the humerus gives rise to this lateral curve, which consequently terminates just below it. When, on the other hand, the deltoid is strongly developed, the most prominent part of the muscle is not that covering the head of the humerus, as there the fibres are all spread out, but immediately below it, where the fibres are converging to their insertion.

The lines which the herculean type of deltoid

muscle offers in its various aspects are not elegant,
but they serve to express enormous physical power,
and may be beautiful just as sheer force is beautiful
when sympathetically treated, as Michelangelo treated
them when dealing with masses of highly-developed
and strongly-accentuated muscles.

On such shoulders as these, where little fat is
present, may be seen peculiar grooves and furrows,
which otherwise are not perceptible on the shoulders.
They follow the direction of the fibres of the deltoid,
and come most clearly into view when it is stimulated
to action, and at the same time prevented by external
resistance from contracting overmuch. They are due
to the flesh of the muscle being divided into good-
sized bundles, whose adjacent surfaces lie more or less
vertically to the skin, and correspond to the said
grooves or furrows.

In the female a thorax which is too broad in its
upper part may be disfiguring, especially if, by reason
of the form of the ribs, its breadth is acquired at the
expense of its depth, that is, at the expense of its
antero-posterior diameter. This is the broad, flat
thorax which is particularly common in the Anglo-
saxon race.

The best female figures have a thorax whose transverse diameter is large enough to join the shoulders
on to it, so that they do not stand apart and form
isolated wing-like structures, so to speak ; but, on the
other hand, it must be neither too large in proportion
to its depth, nor in relation to the diameter of the

upper arms and shoulders.   Shoulders and arms that are narrow in comparison to the extent of the chest have always a poverty-stricken appearance.

Passing fashions must not be allowed to mislead us into thinking that the same does not hold good of the draped figure.   The effect is really just as bad ; only our sense of it is blunted by custom.   We need only go to S. Sebastiano, in Venice, to see what were the views of Tommaso Lombardi on this point.

The breast, in the more restricted meaning of the word (*Mamma*), is somewhat differently placed in different women.   In some it is turned more outwards, so that the nipples are, comparatively speaking, widely separated ; in others they are much closer together, and directed more to the front.   This depends in part on the degree of development of the breast.   The breast in developing draws after it the skin which it requires for its increasingly convex surface, and as the skin on the side of the body yields more readily than that lying between the breasts, the nipples come, at a later period, to lie nearer to each other relatively than they did before the movement consequent on the development commenced.   On this account, and also by reason of the thorax having more slender proportions, the nipples are set closer together in women than in men.   With a given breadth of thorax preference is justly accorded to a wide divergence of the nipples.

" The breasts should always live at enmity with each other," is the remark I once heard from a sculptor; "the right breast should look to the right, and the left to the left." At the same time, the hollow between them must not be too deep, but should slope down gradually to the level of the sternum. If the thorax is well developed in its antero-posterior diameter, this aids the formation of breasts of the above type.

Apart from the foregoing, however, other differences, which equally depend on the structure of the thorax, occur in the position of the breasts among women.

With regard to the height at which the breasts are attached to the body, differences are found bearing no relation to pendulousness arising from their weight or want of consistency, but manifesting themselves at an early stage of development. Among models, in other respects equally good, preference should be given to those having breasts set high up on the thorax. This is invariably the case in antique sculpture.

In the Venus of the Capitol indeed this does not at first sight seem to be so, but the lower position of the breasts must here be attributed in part to their weight, and to the attitude of the whole figure. Un-usually high breasts occur on the so-called Venus Genetrix, No. 265, in the Uffizi.

At first no decided rule prevailed in Italian art. Many painters took the antique as their model; others, however, e.g., Correggio in his Danaë, adopted a lower line of attachment for the breasts. But then this celebrated picture, which has not escaped some very severe censures,* does not make upon us the impression of being an ideal work of art so much as the portrait of a model of whom the master, whether rightly or wrongly, aimed at giving a faithful and realistic representation.

Not, however, until the period of the decline of Italian art is reached, do we find a preference accorded by many masters to a lower attachment of the breasts, such as does, in fact, occur very often in nature.

A like tendency to set the breasts low down is found in certain masters of the German renaissance; the fault being evidently due to the badness of the models they employed. The position of the breasts, considered with reference to the subjacent ribs, undergoes but very slight variation. When, therefore, the ribs about halfway down take an oblique course downwards, the attachment of the breasts will be a low one; but when the arc formed by the ribs does not sink anteriorly, the breasts will lie higher up.

With respect to the shape of the breasts, the first condition is that their lower border shall not be bounded by any trace of a fold, not even when the model is standing upright, with the arms hanging at the side. Antique sculpture knows no such fold in the representation of the nude; where the presence of such a fold might be looked for, the breasts were always covered with drapery. Not until the Italian artists ventured once more to reproduce the naked

* *Cf.* Burckhardt in the " Cicerone."

human form does this fold appear, and its occurrence may be ascribed to the scarcity of girls who could be found to sit as models, and to the constraint and want of freedom with which their forms were copied, owing to the fact that the artists had so little opportunity of observing them.

This serves to explain the low attachment and pendulous, if round, type of breast, bounded below by a hard line, which is found in the renowned Venus of Sandro Botticelli in the Uffizi (Fig. 4, on p. 31).

Later, also, when the domination of the antique models was uncontested, occasional and in part deliberate deviations from the classical type are met with ; as, for instance, in the figure of Eve in the large picture of Angelo Bronzino, the Descent into Hades, in the Uffizi. It is possible that the artist intended to characterise her wifehood and motherhood. But such deviations also occur elsewhere, *e.g.*, in the Three Graces by Francesco Morandini (Uffizi, No. 1,240). One of them has round breasts, the second more conical breasts (the third is only seen in back view), but in both the nipples point downwards, and not, as with the ancients, either forwards, or else forwards and outwards.

The last-named peculiarity is probably due merely to the model selected by Morandini ; with another model he would doubtless have drawn different breasts.

Among the ancients, however, we have to distinguish several forms of breast. To begin with the simplest, the breast may be set on the thorax like a cone, which, if cut through its axis, would exhibit an angle of 90° or more.* The breasts of the Braschi Venus, in the Glyptothek at Munich,† approximate to this type ; and still more do those of a Nymph by Canova, which I saw at Possagno, but of the exact title of which I have unfortunately made no note. This form of breast is never found in women who have borne children, even when they have not suckled them ; because during pregnancy changes take place in the breast affecting its consistency for all later time. It is required of this form that it should scarcely yield at all to the force of gravity, and that its shape should be almost the same in the recumbent as in the upright position. It is excessively rare for breasts of this type to attain any considerable size, since only very occasionally is their consistency sufficiently firm to maintain the form when the dimensions are increased. More frequently such .breasts are found as a transitional stage in young girls. The cone is then smaller and lower down, and

* Though I do not add "or less," I do not mean to assert that this may not occur. On ancient Egyptian monuments we see breasts in which the height is equal to more than half the diameter of the base ; and examples are still to be found, so it is said, among the daughters of the fellaheen ; later these breasts become very limp and pendulous, so much so that occasionally a fellah woman is met with carrying her baby on her back, and suckling it from her breast, which is thrown over the shoulder.

† By some regarded as a free imitation of the Cnidian Aphrodite of Praxiteles, an opinion based on certain coins.

sometimes exhibits at a little distance from the nipple a quite small but somewhat steeper slope, after which the surface of the cone regains its former contour.

From this conical breast we can derive a second type. If the surface of the cone be imagined as bulging out at some distance from the apex, and the nipple on the apex as beginning to raise itself more distinctly from the surrounding area, the whole will tend to assume a form consisting of a hemisphere with the nipple on the top of it.

Before, however, this shape is finally reached, the

FIG. 8.

force of gravity begins to make itself felt, in consequence whereof the lower portion of the former conical surface grows more convex and rounded, and thus we arrive at the form of breast seen in most antique figures of Venus, including those of Medicis and Milo. In Fig. 8 the dotted line shows the rectangular section of the purely conical breast, while the continuous line shows the antique Venus breast derived from it. In various statues the shape is more or less divergent, according as the angle, here drawn as a right angle, exceeds it more or less, and becomes an obtuse angle.

A step further brings us to the breast of the Capitoline Venus. This is larger and heavier, and the increase of heaviness is evident. In my judgment a limit is here reached which should not be exceeded in ideal figures.

Michelangelo's figures have breasts of an essentially different type from the antique. They are more rounded, and more affected by the force of gravity. I am not referring only to the figure of Night, in which the breasts are those of a mature woman, but also to those of the Dawn and of the Leda, assuming that the marble Leda is a genuine work of Michelangelo.* In these figures the breasts could scarcely be replaced by others without disturbing the unity of the whole; taken by themselves alone, however, they fall far behind the antique type. If the figures in question be imagined as made of flesh and blood, and no longer in a recumbent position, but standing upright, this will be admitted by any one who knows the difference between the recumbent and the standing model.

But it was just the hand of the great master which was able to throw any given body into its most favourable form, and which knew how to weave into his magic lines structural details which under any

---

* It is described as such in the Bargello at Florence, but I am not acquainted with the results of antiquarian research touching it. The corresponding picture, of which several examples are extant, must not be confounded with the Leda which Michelangelo painted for Alfonso d'Este—a different composition, as is evident from Vasari's description. This Leda was represented in a wholly different attitude.

other circumstances would have disturbed their harmony.　Michelangelo had also a fondness for separating the breasts by a broad intervening space, and
marking them off from this space by definite lines.
Every breast that is at all movable glides a little on
the subjacent surface, downwards when the model
stands up, and outwards in the recumbent position ;
but this is not the reason why in Michelangelo's
figures the breasts are set so far apart, for, in the first
place, they have not drawn the skin with them to any
remarkable extent, and, secondly, in the figure of Night
the body is so much raised that the shifting ought
to be rather downward than lateral.　The left breast
might possibly be drawn outwards by the retracted
arm, but not so the right breast, the contour of which
is nevertheless sharply defined at some distance from
the sternum.

Widely-separated breasts of this kind do also occur
in the antique, e.g., in the Barberini Venus.　Compare
these with those of the Capitoline Venus.　The great
difference which is here visible cannot be put down to
the attitude alone.

In nature these breasts are seen more especially
in tall women, with a broad thorax which is rather
flattened than well-arched, and with a small round
Mamma ; for the more circumscribed the boundaries
of the breasts, the further apart will they lie on the
broad surface of the thorax ; and the less the sternum,
with its attached costal cartilages, is rounded in
front, the less gradual will be the slope of the breasts

towards the median line, and the sharper will be the boundary line dividing them from the surface on which they lie.

It is not necessary for every breast to commence with a conical shape, and later to grow rounder as its mass enlarges ; it may develop from its origin as a low rounded eminence. Such a breast is seen in the lovely but very mutilated antique in the Naples Museum known as a Psyche. As it is only quoted here for an illustration, it does not concern us whether its present form is the original one or is the result of a later restoration of the statue.*

If we examine the various sculptures of the best period in ancient art, we shall find numerous variations, though none that can be reckoned as defective. As far as the representation of the breast is concerned, the ancients are unsurpassed for delicacy of feeling, and they appear to have had no lack of models.

I will now mention a mode of representing the

* In C. Friederich's "Bausteine zur Geschichte der griechisch-römischen Plastik," I. The Casts in the New Museum at Berlin, at p. 253, we read the following words with reference to the restoration of the Psyche : " Moreover a ruthless reworking of the trunk at least has been carried out, whereby the injured portions, instead of being mended, have simply been chipped away. The breasts, especially the right one, have thereby been rendered quite flat ; further, the right thigh and the drapery have not been left untouched." I cannot trust to my recollections of the original, which are too old and indistinct ; but on examining a good plaster cast, which still retained its seams, I could discover no clear traces of the chiselling away. The figure in its present condition also affords no evidence to justify such an assumption. The right breast is indeed less prominent than the left, but this is

female breast, unknown to antiquity and the renaissance,* but one which may occasionally be seen in
works of art at the present day. The chisel of the
sculptor fashions on each breast a low circular eminence
of from 3 to 3½ centimetres in diameter, gently rising
towards the centre, at which point stands the nipple
erect, while its border is marked off from the skin of
the breast by a rather sharp outline. This elevation
does actually occur, but it may be present or absent
in the same breast at different times. In the nipple
and around it in the so-called areola lies a layer of
muscular fibres which contract very slowly. In doing
so they cause the elevation in question, which disappears on their being relaxed, and the contour of the
nipple then passes, as in the antique, insensibly into
that of the breast.

It is not sufficient, however, to study the form and
position of the breasts alone by themselves ; we must
also consider them in connection with the thorax on

accounted for by the attitude. Perhaps it might be suggested
that the former should be rather more concentrated ; but if there
is an error here, it is one that may just as well be placed to the
account of the original artist as to that of the restorer. The
general flatness of the breasts is here an attribute of youth. If
the figure is to be regarded as a Psyche, then these breasts are,
at any rate, more appropriate to the poetical conception of the
figure than the hemispheres which are given to Psyche in the
Farnesina. There the close adherence to Apuleius always seemed
to me to be overstrained.

* The marks which were observed by Winkelmann round the
nipples of the Antinous of the Belvedere may be related hereto ;
but my memory as to the details of the original is not distinct
enough to allow of my asserting this.

which they lie. A well-arched thorax not only affords the breasts a better position and surface, but also determines the outward form of the whole bust. One of the most frequent faults we meet with in this connection consists in the junction of the ribs with the sternum becoming visible. When not attributable to excessive leanness, this is due to a sickly disposition in childhood, and any model in whom it is perceptible should be rejected forthwith.

Further, no prominence ought to be present on the upper part of the sternum, accompanied below, as it usually is, by a depression between the breasts. This blemish is caused by the *Manubrium sterni*, the portion of the breast-bone lying between the clavicles and first two pairs of ribs, being attached to the meso-sternum, not in a straight line, but at a projecting angle. The effect is equally bad if an inwardly projecting angle is formed at the same point. The clavicles, moreover, ought not to project so as to show where they lie ; least of all should the skin sink in above and behind them, so as to give rise to a pair of pits.

The entire surface extending above the breasts to the neck and shoulders should be gently convex, without any prominent elevations or depressions, and, above all, the transition to the shoulder should be gradual and unbroken. The pit of the neck should be only lightly indicated. It is difficult to lay down any rule as to the line dividing the neck from the breast, as its character is subject to great variation, according as the neck is inclined or set quite upright on the thoracic spinal column.   In the first condition, which is seen in the Venus de Medicis, the Capitoline Venus, that of Milo, and likewise in the Venus of the Esquiline, this boundary line is the softest and least marked, though at the same time the most complete ; in the second case it may be entirely obliterated in front, though more strongly marked at the sides ; and if fatty tissue be present, it may even become a fold lying between two cushions of fat.

Between the breast and the shoulder lies a familiar prominence, constituting in part the anterior wall of the armpit ; it is reproduced with admirable effect in numerous antique sculptures, and especially in the Venus of Milo.   Those artists who take the antique as their pattern are careful to repeat it, since they know how to value the beauty of the line that it offers from different points of view.   It is frequently not to be seen in the living model, because its presence is conditional on three factors which are not always found associated together.   The first of these is the vigorous development of the pectoral muscles, especially of the *M. pectoralis major* ; the second is the presence of a moderate layer of fat, neither overmuch nor too little ; the third factor is a breast with a firm consistency of its own, a breast that neither yields to the force of gravity nor drags on the skin lying between itself and the axilla.

Fig. 9 shows this feature clearly though not strongly developed, from a photograph of the living model.

It is notorious that even those artists who never trouble themselves about the antique frequently make alterations in the breasts, as those of models in other respects well formed and well trained are often no longer in a condition to allow of their being faithfully reproduced. In making such corrections, attention should be likewise paid to the anterior wall of the axilla, and the antique taken as a model.

What has been said above holds good for figures of women who are in the prime of life, and have attained a vigorous development. The artist must learn by

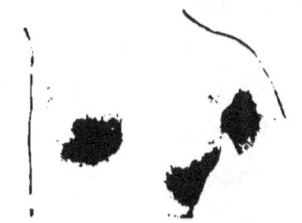

FIG. 9.

experience, from the study of quite young and slender models, how far he should depart from the requirements insisted on above, when his object is to represent the opening blossom of beauty. He must be very careful, however, not to confound development that is incomplete, though normally healthy, with meagre and sickly development. Above all, he must guard against attempting to give an impression of youth by a thorax of poverty-stricken proportions; for a normal well-developed thorax differs from an ill-developed one in youth just as much as in later life, even if it is not quite similar to that of the adult.

It is well not to place too much confidence in the
models that present themselves, especially in Germany,
as the German thorax is far oftener badly developed
than the thorax in the Latin race. Nevertheless, in
Italy also defects are met with in this respect. One
that I have often observed since, I was first struck
with in a graceful figure of Innocence of Milanese
origin. This defect consists in a depression below
the breast, just beneath the mammary gland, and is
always associated with a poorly-developed thorax. I
do not intend to dilate here on the ravages committed
by the corset in giving a modified and wholly unnatural shape to all the lower part of the thorax.
Unhappily the corset is often worn at an early age, in
order, as mothers foolishly express it, " to form the
figure." It is just those girls who during the period
of their development have no waist, and in whom,
therefore, the lower part of the thorax is full and
round, that grow up with the most beautiful figures.
They get rid later of their temporary squareness by
upward growth.

Let us now pass on to the shoulders. Apart from
their being placed too high or too low, their commonest defect consists in an imperfectly-developed
deltoid muscle. This blemish is partly inherent in
the race, but in part, also, it arises from the fact that
in the female portion of the middle and upper classes
the muscles are very little exercised, and the deltoid
least of all. This muscle is brought into play when
the arm is raised high above the head—as, for instance,

in picking apples from a tree when one is standing on the ground, or in hanging up linen on the drying lines, or in supporting a burden which is being carried on the head, or in raising a weight above the head.

These, however, are movements which girls of the higher classes seldom have occasion to perform, and which, even if it were the fashion, they would be prevented from executing by the nature of the clothes in which, from an early age, they are attired. Such are the bodices in which the shoulderpiece does not rest on the upper bony portion of the shoulder, but is carried right across the deltoid muscle. If a girl so dressed tries to lift her right arm up into the air, she has to bend the upper part of her body to the left, because it is only with difficulty that she can make an obtuse angle between her arm and her body. When the deltoid is badly developed, the shoulders, unless well provided with fat, are angular above, owing to the prominence of the bony framework formed by the distal end of the clavicle and the free end of the scapular spine, the acromion. From this angular summit the surfaces then fall away without the required amount of convexity. The addition of fat may improve the shape, but it will never achieve that beautiful roundness which in well-modelled shoulders converts them into something more than the mere upper end of an arm. Rauch's celebrated wreath-throwing Victories, so well known through countless reproductions, with all their beauty have a weak and meagre look about the shoulders.

Whether it be owing to the race, or the habit of carrying and supporting light burdens on the head, Italy produces far more well-formed shoulders in women than Germany, and evidence of this may be found in Italian art. If any one desires a striking illustration of the difference between German and Italian types, let him compare the slender form of the Herodias of Vincenzo Dati, in the Baptistery of the Cathedral at Florence, with the above-mentioned Victories of Rauch. Even in the delicately-formed Madonna of Mino da Fiesole, in the Cathedral of Fiesole, the shoulders are vigorously developed. Indeed, it is not too much to say that the art of the renaissance attached more importance to well-formed shoulders than that of antiquity; at any rate the deltoid becomes more marked in the former, since during the renaissance, especially in the earlier part of that period, the upper arm was represented as less fat and less cylindrical than it is in classical works of art.

Not exactly on the summit of the shoulder, but a little behind it, may sometimes be seen a small fossa, which, when the arm is lifted upwards and backwards, becomes a crescent-shaped depression. The latter is also found in other individuals as the result of the same movements. It arises in consequence of the contraction of the deltoid, which swells up, while the bones to which it is attached remain deep below. In some persons, however, a small fossa remains visible when the arm hangs loosely at the side. As this is rather rare, the fossa does not form part of the general impression which the memory retains of a well-formed shoulder. Therefore the artist cannot exactly be required to reproduce it. On the other hand, it is no disfigurement, no defect of beauty, and is present only in individuals having vigorous muscles and a skin well knit to the subjacent tissues.

IV.

THE ABDOMEN.

THE abdomen in the male is of value in art in proportion as it is small in size and exhibits certain normal details.

Smallness of the abdomen in healthy men in the prime of life is mainly conditional on its not being distended by large masses of food and gaseous products; but it also depends on whether the iliac crests are very widely separated or not, since they determine the width of the lower portion of the abdomen, by providing points of insertion for the abdominal muscles.

Inhabitants of southern countries generally have a smaller abdomen than men of the north, because they are satisfied from their youth upwards with a less amount of nourishment; and the children of the richer classes have usually a smaller one than those of the poor, as they are brought up on more nutritious and therefore less bulky fare. For the rest, the condition of the health and individual development are the factors chiefly concerned. When the abdomen has to harbour large masses of digested and undigested food-stuffs, and intestinal gases are present in quantity and the abdominal muscles are not powerfully developed, the form of the abdomen is always bad.

To enter more into detail, the primary condition is that the depression corresponding to the tendinous portion of the abdominal wall between the recti and oblique muscles be visible. As this is a depression and not a furrow, its course cannot be laid down with rigid definiteness, but it may be found by dividing the abdomen across into four equal parts at the height of the navel, when the first vertical dividing line on either side of the navel will coincide with the depression in question. It is seen to descend from above in a nearly vertical line, then bend slightly inwards, so that, if still visible at the upper border of the pelvic region, its course may be pursued downwards at a little distance to the inside of the anterior superior iliac spine. This lower portion, however, is often indistinct, though the model cannot merely on that account be regarded as useless. A well-rounded base to the thorax contributes materially to the definiteness of this depression in its upper part. The arched character of that region is derived from the ascending processes of the recti muscles ; then on either side is a lateral elevation formed by the external oblique muscles which descend from the ribs, and between these two the depression in question has its origin at the base of the thorax. If the cartilaginous ribs are too much bent out in this region, the form of the abdomen suffers in consequence.

The median line of the body has to be mentioned next. In muscular persons a depression is seen running along the sternum between the points of origin of the great pectoral muscles. Starting from this it is possible to trace the median line, with more or less interruption, down to the navel. In female antique statues it does not form a groove beyond this point, but in heroic figures it is often indicated also between the navel and the pubic prominence.

This groove, which corresponds to the tendinous band between the recti muscles of each side, called the *linea alba*, varies in distinctness according to the attitude,* and may be entirely absent in the female, including the upper portion, without the model being thereby rendered unserviceable. For instance, to judge from a photograph lying before me, it would appear to be invisible in the Venus of the Esquiline. When it does occur, however, in the model, the artist

---

* The appearance of the groove is, especially in its lower portion, dependent chiefly on the action of a muscle, the pyramidal muscle of the abdomen, which takes its origin from the two pubic bones on either side of the symphysis, and also from the symphysis itself. Its fibres run on either side upwards and slightly inwards towards the median line, and are inserted into the fibrous tissue of the *linea alba*. When therefore they contract, they draw the *linea alba* downwards, and stretch it in doing so. In the process the *linea alba* sinks down amid the surrounding structures, and so gives rise to a groove on the surface, as it tends to form a straight line, extending from the ensiform process of the sternum to the symphysis pubis. The main reason why this groove is less often visible in women, and cannot be traced so far down, is that the abdominal wall is more richly supplied with fat, partly also that the muscles are less strongly developed.

should be careful to copy it. Otherwise he will not merely deprive his figure of an ornament, but also suppress a feature by means of which the expression of its action might be much enhanced.

Sometimes a line is visible, even in the upright position, lying transversely at some distance above the navel, or, in lieu thereof, a pair of transverse depressions lying on either side external to the recti muscles, and meeting at right angles to the longitudinal groove above described. This line corresponds to the crease or fold which is formed when a person standing upright leans forward, or sits in a leaning attitude. In individuals who are at once muscular and wanting in fat, several tendinous bands of the recti muscles of the abdomen, known as the *inscribtiones tendineæ*, may be visible at the surface. They are often defined in antique sculpture to a degree that we are scarcely acquainted with in the ordinary model. We must, however, recollect that the sculptors of ancient times probably had opportunities of making observations on famous athletes, such as we no longer possess. That these transverse creases may also be visible in thin individuals of only moderate muscular power is evident from the annexed copy of a photograph from the life (Fig. 10).

The limits of the abdomen towards the thorax vary very much with the attitude, differing according as the modelling of the lower thoracic region is prominent in its anterior central portion, or is obliterated through the stretching of the recti muscles which are attached to the cartilages of the fifth to the seventh rib, and to the lateral portions of the ensiform process. The latter takes place more especially when the hip-joint of the supporting leg is over-extended, so as to cause the ilio-femoral ligament to be stretched; and, the obliquity of the pelvis being slight, equilibrium is restored by a forward movement of the pelvis.

In order that all these details may be visible, the

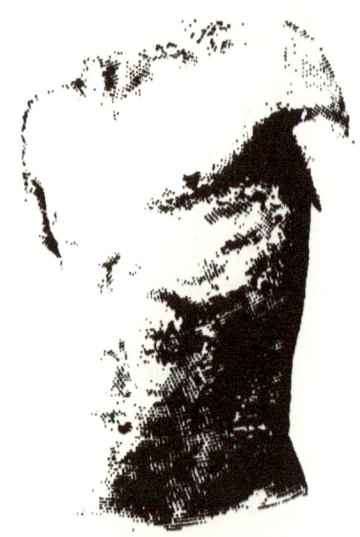

FIG. 10.

abdomen must not be overloaded with fat. But ideal male figures are seldom represented as having much fat. Some figures of Bacchus, which, in spite of their youthful beauty, display a certain fullness of form, are an exception to this rule; but even then the fat layer must not be such as to obliterate entirely the details of the modelling of the abdomen, but only such as to soften them and render them less prominent.

The fat layer of the abdomen must, in general, not

exceed the proportion found in the softer parts of the rest of the body. Regard must always be had to the conditions of youth, and care taken not to approximate to the type of older men, in whom the amount of abdominal fat has increased relatively to that of the arms and legs.

Just as absence of fat, to a certain degree, from the abdomen is becoming in the male, so leanness, in the ordinary sense of the word, *i.e.*, leanness arising from a poverty of muscular development, is very prejudicial. In the latter case, the abdomen is not only bad from want of definition, and movement called forth by the muscles, but its lower portion is further disfigured by the prominence of the iliac crests.

We are, by reason of our models and observations made in bathing resorts, so accustomed to see male figures with poorly-developed muscles and an ill-conditioned thorax, that we are constantly tempted to charge the ancients with exaggeration. The prominences especially on the upper region of the abdomen, and on the lower part of the thorax, are frequently stated to be mere figments of their imagination. But we should be cautious in passing such judgments. The accompanying woodcut (Fig. 11), drawn from the photograph of a powerful but by no means herculean man, should be considered. Here we see the same features exposed to view as in the ancient heroic figures, only less strongly marked. May not the ancients have had models in whom they noted the details that they reproduced in marble?

What shape ought to be given to the navel ? We may distinguish between a projecting and a depressed navel. The former was not unknown to the Greeks, though they gave the preference to the latter. The Ægina marbles, indeed, exhibit a moderately-convex navel ; its convexity, however, is so much sunk below the surrounding surface, as not to project beyond the level of the abdominal wall.

FIG. 11.

As a matter of fact, not only is the convex navel at the present time the rarer form, but also the less agreeable, as in it the umbilical ring is less perfectly closed than in the depressed form. Were the closure more imperfect still, and the umbilical ring yet wider, a pathological condition known as umbilical hernia would exist. However, even when this condition is not present, it is possible to feel with the finger the border of the incompletely-closed umbilical ring. In the recumbent position the convex navel sinks in, or, at any rate, can be easily pressed down. In the upright position, however, or if subjected to the pressure of muscular contraction, as during an action of the bowels, the umbilicus becomes prominent once more ; and its imperfect closure, and the communication with the abdominal cavity, are thereby rendered manifest.

The position of the umbilicus should not be determined with reference to the vertical proportions of the whole figure, as is frequently done by artists who make use of certain systems of measurement in which the navel serves as the central point. The result is to place it too high in short-legged and too low in long-legged persons. The position of the navel has nothing to do with the length of the legs, and should be determined solely with reference to the proportions of the trunk. It has a better effect when placed relatively high rather than low down. Ordinarily the umbilicus is situated higher up when the obliquity of the pelvis is slight than when it is pronounced.

The same principles apply in general to the female abdomen, but at the outset we have to deal with a larger amount of fat. A rounded and somewhat prominent abdomen, of a form not found in women of more mature age, is by some regarded as a characteristic of virginal beauty. If, however, an attempt is made to translate it into marble or bronze, as has frequently been done, the result at once proves how ill-advised such an attempt is. Many such figures are met with in the art of the German renaissance, but the impression they produce is not a pleasing one.

Success in this respect is equally difficult to painters, who in others may claim to take greater liberties. Even so great a master as Giovanni Bellini is an instance. Can any one look at his allegorical figure, No. 236 in the Pinacoteca Contarini (Venice, Accademia delle Belle Arti), with entire satisfaction? It is conceivable, however, that the artist intended here to represent the woman as *enceinte*. The name given to the figure in art histories, *La nuda verità*, might then be appropriately rendered as Sincerity. This is not impossible, as she holds in her hand a *tondo*, in which is mirrored the face of a man.

In a model that shall be adapted for ideal figures, the two longitudinal depressions, which I have mentioned above in treating of the male figure, ought to be visible on the outside of the sheath of the recti abdominis muscles. Lower down they pass in the female subject into a kind of flat depression or valley, the superior elevated boundary of which forms a circle, having for its centre or close thereto the umbilicus. This valley is bounded inferiorly by the iliac furrow at the sides, while in the centre it descends to a second elevation, the pubic prominence, or *mons Veneris*.

The circular elevation round the umbilicus is caused by a layer of fat generally present in women, such as also occurs in greater or less quantity in the mons

veneris. If the artist holds faithfully to the configuration above described, he will not so readily lose his way
in contours that are often difficult to understand.

It should, however, be mentioned that the groove
between the abdomen and the pubic prominence is
frequently very shallow in slender youthful forms.
This cannot justly be regarded as a defect. In the
Venus rising from the Sea of Sandro Botticelli (Uffizi,
Florence) it is well marked, although doubtless faithfully copied from a long and slender model; little trace
of it, however, is to be seen in the Graces in the Opera
del Duomo at Siena. The Venus of the Esquiline,
likewise a youthful figure, though revealing a smaller
and fuller type of model, shows it in a marked degree.
It is, perhaps, somewhat emphasized here by the
attitude; but it is not due to this cause alone, since
it is more marked than in the Capitoline Venus, who
is also bending forward and is evidently a woman
of more mature development. The contours of the
maiden's abdomen are spoilt by pregnancy and
childbirth. As a consequence, the abdominal walls
occasionally become so thin and flaccid that the shape
of the subjacent coils of the intestine is visible on the
surface and their movements perceptible.

Even when this is not the case, either the fat
disappears from the umbilical region or is absorbed in
a general adipose layer more evenly distributed over
the whole abdomen, though it may be thickest at a
short distance round the navel.

After the tension which the skin and subjacent

connective tissue undergo during pregnancy they
seldom recover their former firmness, and thus it
becomes intelligible that the fat deposited in them is
no longer held in position so rigidly as before. When
present in considerable quantity it draws the skin of
the abdomen after it by its weight, and so tends to
make it pendulous.

Such far-reaching changes are, however, by no means
the rule ; and indeed the mere fact of childbirth need
not permanently disfigure the abdomen. The so-called
scars of pregnancy—that is, scar-like depressions in
the lower abdominal and inguinal region, of oblong,
mostly rhombic form—are ordinarily though not
always present. Less often a brown line, called the
linea fusca, is seen ascending from the mons veneris
towards the umbilicus. But these and other disfigure-
ments may disappear after a time ; and indeed this
may be the case to such a degree that the medical man,
who has to give his opinion in a court of justice as to
whether a woman has been a mother or not, might be
left in doubt in some cases by the general aspect of
the abdomen, if a closer examination of the genital
organs did not furnish a conclusive answer. This is
a well-known fact in forensic medicine.

The bust, it is true, never regains the ideal shape of
youth, but the modifications it undergoes furnish no
guidance to the medical expert, unless unmistakable
changes have taken place in the nipples or in the
areola. Every artist of experience knows well enough
that the breasts often leave very much to be desired,

even in young models who have never been mothers.
Their early deterioration is the result partly of the
natural looseness of the connective tissue associated
with so extensive a glandular mass, and partly of a
want of compactness in the skin, and partly also of
emaciation following previous deposition of fat, or it
may be of a fresh deposit of fatty material. However
good her apparent recovery, a model who has once
been a mother is always to be accepted with great
caution (except when required only for some particular
portion of the body) when the artist has an ideal
figure in view, even where we are purposely left in
doubt as to whether it represents a girl or a married
woman. A model of this kind should be chosen only
when it is desired to stamp the figure with the character of wifehood or motherhood—as, for instance, in
Michelangelo's Night and in various figures of Eve,
where this has been carried out with an evident
purpose.

A material and peculiarly objectionable disfigurement of the female abdomen is caused by the
premature use of the corset. In the first place, the
natural form of the thorax in its lower part and of
the upper part of the abdomen is destroyed ; and, in
addition, the flanks are ruined by being laced up.
The line of the flank from the waist should form a
convex curve, either unbroken and continuous with
the line of the thigh down to the great trochanter,
or it should form a slight elevation above the iliac
crest, with a very shallow depression just below it.

But when the flanks have been disfigured by lacing, the iliac crest projects as a ridge, which may be conspicuous as far as to the anterior superior iliac spine. A still more obvious disfigurement consists in the skin and fat of the abdomen being pressed downwards, and forming a swelling over the border of the pelvis, which extends farther down laterally than in the centre. These deformities may be observed even in the corpse ; and just below the swelling that is formed in the centre, the scalpel comes upon the *M. pyramidalis abdominis*. It is to the activity of this muscle that the strangely ugly form assumed by this disfigurement seems to be due.

A low umbilicus produces a still more unpleasant effect in the female than in the male. Its position is defined most conveniently by comparing its distance from the pit of the neck, that is, from the upper end of the sternum, with its distance from the point where the lines of the flexure of the thighs meet at the apex of the fork.

If the latter distance be taken as 100, the former is equal to 174 in the Graces of the Opera del Duomo at Siena, and the same in the Venus of the Vatican, who holds up her hair with her right hand, and in her left carries a vase for unguents. In Sandro Botticelli's Venus it amounts to 167 ; in a woman 5 feet 3½ inches high, whose measurement was taken by Schadow, to 162 ; in the Venus de Medicis, calculated by him for the erect position, to 160 ; and in a woman 5 feet 6 inches high measured by him only to 157. The artist is free to make his choice among these ratios, for even in the Graces at Siena the umbilicus is not unduly low, though its position would be no longer tolerable if the line of the flexure of the thighs, both in them and in the above-named Venus, made a less obtuse angle.

Where the boundary line between the abdomen and the pubic prominence is visible in the upright posture, a very common practice is to carry a straight line from its lowest point to the fossa of the neck, and to fix the umbilicus on it at such a point that its distance from the fossa of the neck is the double of that from the lowest point of the boundary line aforesaid.

The position of the umbilicus is, however, materially dependent in one and the same individual on that of the body. When the body is bent on the thighs, and therefore the obliquity of the pelvis is increased, the umbilicus descends ; while the opposite takes place when the obliquity of the pelvis is much diminished, so as to bring the ilio-femoral ligament into a state of tension. If, however, the spinal column is flexed in bending the body, which takes place mainly in the lumbar vertebræ, the umbilicus shifts relatively upwards, since the sternum is brought closer to it, and so the distance between the umbilicus and the pit of the neck is diminished.

When the body is bent forwards in the lumbar region, a transverse crease is formed on the abdominal wall above the navel; as seen, for example, in the so-called Danaid of the Vatican—in which, however, be it said in passing, I can only see the figure of a woman about to perform her ablutions (Fig. 12). It is also excellently shown in the beautiful figure of Susannah, in Lauritz Tuxen's picture of Susannah at the Bath. In Fig. 13 an example of it is given from a photograph of a female model.

The same crease is produced when the body is bent forward in the sitting position. It is caused by the lowest part of the thorax, together with the

FIG. 12.

lumbar vertebræ, moving backwards, and drawing the abdominal wall after it. In girls who are young and thin it is simply a crease, below which the abdomen rises into a rounded elevation, while the skin above it forms a flat surface, being stretched across from one side of the thorax to the other.

When, however, a larger quantity of fat is present, a fold rather than a crease is formed ; and this is also the rule in every fairly-well-covered frame, though no rule is without its exceptions. When it does not occur as a fold in a body whose contours are otherwise well rounded enough for the purposes of the artist, but appears quite distinctly as a crease, it should be regarded as an essential mark of beauty; and it has been so accepted by artists of reputation, as, for example, by Moretto of Brescia in his Venus Lamenting the Dead Adonis, No. 592 in the Uffizi.*

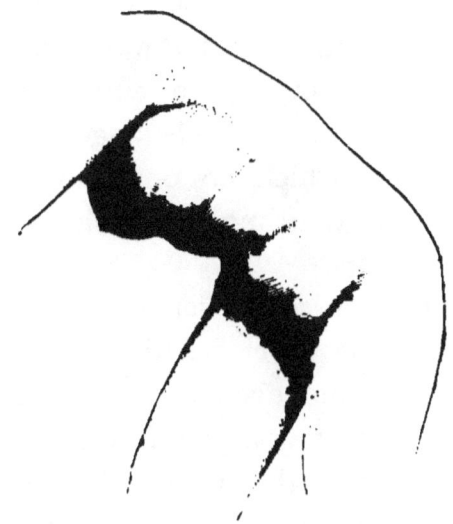

FIG. 13.

A second fold frequently, though not invariably, makes its appearance when the fat is still more conspicuously present; it runs right and left from the navel for a short distance only. If still more fat lies between the sternum and umbilicus, or if the skin

* With reference to the authorship of this picture, I have retained the attribution of the Catalogue. Crowe and Cavalcaselle and Lermolieff agree in ascribing it to Sebastiano Luciani.

is unusually slack, two folds may be formed above the navel in place of the single one first mentioned. Their number may even be still further increased in women who have borne children ; but artists should not suffer themselves to be misled into reproducing an abdomen marked with numerous folds—not even by Michelangelo's Night, which has four transverse abdominal folds, two above and two below the navel. In this instance the sculptor was not concerned to represent ideal beauty, but to emphasize the characteristics of maternity. Michelangelo has done this with a boldness which no one can be encouraged to imitate who does not also share the master's marvellous powers.

Grooves, creases, and even folds running between the navel and the lower pelvic boundary line, must never be copied, not even if present in models who are young and otherwise well-formed ; since they are not associated with the normal development of the human body, but are the consequence of prejudicial forms of clothing, and, above all, of the use of stays.

V.

THE BACK.

THREE things are of cardinal importance in determining the beauty of the back : the curve of the spinal column, the position of the shoulder-blades, and the shape of the thorax. The curve of the spinal column varies with the posture of the body, but only to a limited extent in the thoracic region. Apart from minute variations caused by the respiratory movements, the curve in that region is fairly constant, especially in old people. This is a consequence of each separate vertebra being conjoined to the whole framework of the thorax, the individual parts of which grow less flexible with advancing years. The principal movements take place in the cervical and lumbar regions of the spinal column, in the latter of which regions the power of movement diminishes rapidly upwards towards the thorax, the lower vertebræ of which, in their turn, are more mobile than the upper ones.

This restriction of mobility to the lumbar region is related principally to the actions of arching and drawing in the back. Lateral and rotatory movements give rise in addition to alterations of form in other parts (*cf.* Langer, *loc. cit.*, p. 181). The form of the curve of the human spinal column in the erect posture is so well known that I need not enter into detail here. It is chiefly a question of the degree of curvature ; and in this point antique statues dating from the best period of Greek sculpture down to the decline of pagan art in Rome may be taken as a pattern. In a few examples of archaic Greek art, such as the Apollo of Tenea, the concavity of the lumbar region of the spinal column is exaggerated to a degree unsuited for imitation. In part, perhaps, it arises from the stiff and rigidly-upright posture of the figure. The more erect the body is, the farther is the centre of gravity shifted backwards. The vertical line, however, drawn through the centre of gravity of course must not fall behind the heels, otherwise the erect posture would be impossible. Therefore the lumbar region of the spinal column is bent in, and thus the central mass of the trunk is shifted farther forwards to make a counterpoise. The military maxim to put in the stomach and stick out the chest is no natural position, but one that has to be acquired by drilling.

The masters of the renaissance period frequently went beyond the antique pattern in this matter of the curvature of the spinal column, but it is not on that account desirable to imitate them. It is, in any case, difficult to lay down any very definite rule, since, owing to the important part often played by the line of the spinal column of a figure in the main lines of a composition, a more marked curve may occasionally be justified under the circumstances.

The more flexibility the model has in the thoracic region of the spinal column, the better it is. This is especially the case with regard to lateral flexibility. The latter is unaffected by the respiratory movements, but comes into play when the shoulders are raised and lowered, *e.g.*, in lifting up the right arm to reach some object, such as fruit, placed on high, while the left arm hangs down and bears a moderate burden, as, for instance, a basket half filled with fruit. In such a case, the more the lateral flexibility of the spinal column is retained, the more charming is the curved line of the backbone resulting from the action. An instance of it may be seen in Giovanni da Bologna's Roman carrying off a Sabine Woman (Florence, Loggia dei Lanzi).

Furthermore, the power of rotating the spinal column on itself, so that the transverse axis of the body through the shoulders no longer lies in the same plane with that through the pelvis, diminishes with age, and it is always an advantage for a model to retain this power in a high degree.

The next point that may be regarded as essential to the beauty of the back is the position of the shoulder-blades. As a matter of course, in very muscular persons the shoulder-blades, by reason of their strongly developed muscles, form a considerable prominence on either side of the spinal column, as may be seen in the executioner who is turning his back in Raffaelle's Judgment of Solomon in the Vatican. This is not inconsistent with beauty, provided that these prominences are connected with the median groove of the back and with the neck by the muscles attached to the posterior border, or the superior angle, or to the spine of the scapula, in such a way as to form an organic whole. We are, however, concerned with a different point. In many persons the posterior edge of the scapula becomes conspicuous by drawing the attached muscles with it, and forming under the skin a roof-shaped prominence, which constitutes a very ugly feature. When in such a case the arm is allowed to hang loosely down, the edge of the bone is seen to be directed obliquely, and the lower angle projects in a most ungraceful fashion. This is by no means merely the result of leanness. In some very lean individuals it is not found at all, while, on the other hand, the objectionable position of the shoulder-blade may make itself visible through a considerable fat layer.

A lean back, one that is free from fat, may be faultless, and this not only in the male, but in the female also ; in the latter case, however, it must present a surface in which there may be depressions, but no projections. At first sight this may seem like a contradiction, and it may be objected that there can be no valleys without hills. But the contradiction is apparent only. Any one who knows how to describe a stretch of country will draw a distinction between a plain from which rise separate hills or chains of hills, and a plain which is scored by single valleys or depressions. It reduces itself to this, that the characteristic features in the one case project above the general level, while in the other they sink below it. In a lean back of this type the play of the muscles will be visible under the skin, but no projecting angles or edges of the bones. I must repeat here that by a lean back I understand merely one that is free from fat ; for a back in which the muscles are not adequately developed is, under all circumstances, ugly.

Where a well-formed back is overlaid with a moderate cushion of fat, there may generally be seen on either side of the median groove, in the region of the shoulders, a shallow longitudinal depression running from above downwards, a longitudinal pit. This pit corresponds to a depression near the hinder border of the scapula, which lies between the point of origin of the infraspinatus muscle on the one hand, and the insertion of the great rhomboid muscle (*M. rhomboideus major*) on the other. Although covered not only by the skin and fat layer, but also by the fibres of the trapezius, it is nevertheless frequently visible at the surface, and should be carefully reproduced, as it is of great importance in the distribution of the surface of the back, and helps to break its monotony. Its presence also affords evidence of a well-developed muscular system, as its depth increases in proportion to the prominence of the surrounding muscles.

This pit is seen most clearly when the arm is actively rotated in the shoulder-joint outwards, be-

cause then the infra-spinatus muscle contracts and
thickens. On the other hand, it is smoothed away
when the arms are folded in front, because the upper
arm in doing so revolves to the inside, and at the
same time, by shifting the shoulders forwards, stretches
and flattens out the rhomboid muscle.

The third material element in the beauty of the
back is the shape of the thorax, which must neither
be abnormally conical in form from above downwards,
nor have its circumference unnaturally narrow in its
lower region. The latter is frequently the case in
the female sex, as the result of wearing a corset at
an early age. I lay stress on the early age, as this
is far more injurious than using such an arrangement
when growth in height and girth is completed. As
regards height, the limit, as is well known, is reached
much sooner than in relation to girth. For the
latter no limit under fifty years of age can be regarded as certainly definite, since not only the bones,
but the soft parts also, are concerned. · The latter
element, however, does not here enter into consideration, as no increase of girth by deposit of fat
is in question, but only addition to the width of
the shoulders and loins through bone-growth, and
this usually ceases among us in the female sex at
twenty years of age, or a little earlier. If the use of
stays is first adopted at this period of life, it cannot
spoil the shape of the back very speedily—at any rate
not during the time in which the individual is likely
to sit as a model. Under these circumstances it

suffices to lay aside the stays for a short time in order to restore the original shape. The same statement cannot be made with equal certainty as regards the abdomen, which, even at the later stage of life, is easily disfigured permanently, especially by the formation of one or more disagreeable transverse folds in the lower abdominal region. Still worse are the ravages inflicted by the corset, not only on the abdomen, but also on the back of those who wear it before or during their development, and make use of it for the purposes of personal display. Girls who do this are quite useless as models.

The tightly-laced body is at once recognisable in back view by the contraction which manifests itself on either side of the spinal column in the lower thoracic region, and by the dwindling resulting therefrom, forming, as the eye descends, a violent contrast with the hips, which, owing to their bony framework, maintain their original position.

Such a back is repulsively ugly, and it would be scarcely conceivable that any artist could think of reproducing it, were it not that examples of it are to be found.

As a rule one hears artists less frequently lament the lack of good models for the back than the absence of those who are good for the breast, abdomen, or feet. This is natural, since, with the exception of the use of stays and the habit of suspending heavy dresses from the hips, the life of most girls at the present day does not involve conditions productive of injury to the back ; and whereas the abdomen and breast only too easily forfeit their beauty with increasing years, this does not apply, in anything like the same degree, to the back.

Among the ancients we often meet with a somewhat

FIG. 14.

rounded back and a forward inclination of the neck— an attitude not regarded as elegant in the draped figure of a girl. The erect bearing required of girls at the present day does not occur with any frequency in art till the Roman period.

The annexed woodcut (Fig. 14), from an engraving

in "Gorii Mus. Florentinum," vol. ii., represents the bust of the goddess Roma cut on a sardonyx. The pose is very characteristic; and the thorax exhibits a roundness which is rare in Greek sculpture.

The pose of the neck in Greek female figures is partly due to the desire to show it off to the highest advantage, as has been mentioned above in the passage relating thereto. Distinctions were also drawn by the ancients themselves in this matter. The afore-mentioned pose of the neck is found chiefly in statues of Venus and in genre figures, whereas figures of Juno and Minerva stand more proudly erect. Archaic and archaistic figures are similarly distinguished by a more upright and, if occasionally stiff, yet frequently solemn and imposing bearing.

If we look at the back of an individual or of a statue in the upright posture, we can easily trace the line of the backbone as it descends between the shoulders downwards, until it is lost in the sacral region, where we see on each side, at a little distance, a depression longer than it is broad; these pits are more or less oblong from above downwards. The elevated masses which lie between them and the line of the backbone consist of the lower part of the dorsal muscles which are attached to the sacrum, and in part, too, of the overlying fat.

From each of these pits there runs obliquely downwards and inwards a line towards the cleft between the buttocks, where the two lines meet. They are either traceable through their entire course, or they are so far indicated as to be easily completed in imagination. What lies above and to the inside of them forms part of the dorsal muscles, and of their tendons and processes; what lies below and outside them belongs to the gluteus muscles. These lines form two sides of a triangle, defined above towards the back more or less distinctly, according to the degree of inclination of the body, and known as the sacro-iliac triangle. It varies in form according to the inclination of the pelvis, according to the form of the sacrum and of the adjacent iliac bones, and according to the extent of the fatty layer. It may present a convex surface to the view, or it may be flat; it may, in addition, exhibit a median or two lateral depressions; but, in any case, it must be recognised by the artist and intelligently worked out in its details, where he is dealing with a youthful and well-preserved body in dorsal view, whether in the male or in the female.

It is very beautifully shown in that one of the Three Graces of Raffaelle who turns her back to the spectator.

It is also well reproduced in Forster's engraving after this picture, which has been spread broadcast by means of the " Blätter für vervielfaltigende Kunst."

I cannot understand the palpable neglect with which this region has been treated in one of the finest statues of antiquity, the Venus of the Capitol. We are almost compelled to suppose that in its original position the back was not accessible to observation. I judge so from the plaster cast which is in the Academy of Fine Arts at Vienna. Since I first observed this I have had no opportunity of examining the original.

VI.

WHEN we look at antique male statues, we observe a striking uniformity in the course of the iliac line—the line, that is, running downwards from the hips towards the genital organs. It is practically identical in archaic statues, in works belonging to the finest period of Greek sculpture, and in examples of Roman plastic art from the time of the Emperors down to the complete decline of pagan art.

Nevertheless, it is not very easy to find in the living model instances of this line, which was persistently reproduced through so many centuries in ancient times. In the first place, where in the antique we see a more or less prominent roll of flesh lying above the iliac crest, we usually find none in well-proportioned young men of slender build, such as are represented in antique statues and reliefs, but frequently in lieu thereof a depression, situated, however, a little higher than the fleshy ridge of the antique; for the latter, as we shall see hereafter, includes the iliac crest, whereas the depression which we meet with in the living subject always lies above the level of the iliac crest.

The difference just referred to is connected with a second one no less remarkable. If we have a living model before us, we observe that the iliac line descending from the iliac crest makes a slight curve as it follows the course of the inguinal fold, *i.e.*, of the fold which, when we bend the thigh, and at the

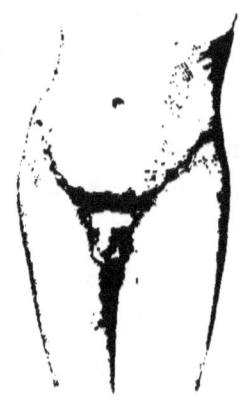

FIG. 15.

same time turn it inwards towards the median plane of the body, is formed between its inner border and the lower abdominal region ; lower down the line is lost in the pubic hair. As its continuation, but no longer as forming part of the iliac line itself, we may regard the line which descends between the thigh and the scrotum and forms the border line between the former and the perinæum, *i.e.*, the region between the scrotum and the anus.

In antique sculpture, however, the line descending

from the hips has a very different shape. It commences with an almost horizontal portion beneath the fleshy ridge, runs for a short distance inwards, and then bends downwards at an obtuse angle, sometimes almost at a right angle ; and pursues a curve convex on the outside and below. The annexed woodcuts illustrate the two forms of line.

FIG. 16.

Figs. 15 and 16 show the ordinary iliac line from photographs of models, the original of Fig. 15 having both hands raised, that of Fig. 16 holding a vase in the right hand. Fig. 17, taken from Sybel's " Weltgeschichte der Kunst," shows the iliac line of the Diadumenos.

Before entering into further detail as to the differences between the antique and the living model, it will be convenient to examine how far the inclination

of the pelvis exercises any influence on the iliac line
in the male.

If a man stands erect, firmly planted on both feet,
at the same time exerting as little muscular effort as
possible, the hip-joint is always a little over-extended.
If we imagine the body to be lifeless, and if while
holding the legs firmly in the above position we
were to make an incision from the front surface

Fig. 17.

inwards towards the neck of the femur, cutting
through everything, skin, muscles, vessels, nerves, and
finally also the anterior wall of the fibrous capsule
of the joint by which the femur is attached to the
pelvis, the trunk would fall backwards. Now, very
strong bundles of fibres run in the anterior wall of
this capsule, which take their origin from the superior
or iliac portion of the border of the acetabulum, and
from thence upwards as far as the anterior inferior
iliac spine; and, becoming united in front of the

head and neck of the femur, take a downward course to the point of their attachment on the anterior inter-trochanteric line of the femur.

These bundles are known collectively as the ilio-femoral ligament ; and it is this ligament which, when in standing upright we avoid all muscular exertion not absolutely necessary, keeps the body from falling backwards, so that it is said, not without reason, that, when standing in the easiest possible position, we use no muscular action to support the body, but suspend it in the hip-joint to the ilio-femoral ligament.

It is owing to the presence of this ligament that no one, not even the most supple ballet-dancer, can extend the leg horizontally backwards without bending the body well forwards.

On the length of this ligament, and on the amount of play it allows, depends, moreover, the position assumed by the pelvis in relation to the thigh and to the horizon in an easy upright posture.* If it allows considerable freedom of movement, then the superior opening or inlet of the pelvis is turned more vertically upwards ; but more to the front, when the ligament is short, and consequently the freedom of movement is restricted. In the former case we speak

* It has recently been incorrectly asserted that no position actually exists in which the ilio-femoral ligament is stretched, and that it is merely a theoretical abstraction. Any model may, however, be placed in such a position, even though it be not one which is assumed naturally by everybody, and will afford conclusive proof that a number of antique statues are so posed.

of a slight inclination, in the latter of a strong inclination of the pelvis. Among us an excessive inclination of the pelvis, especially in the female sex, is a more frequent defect than the reverse. When the inclination is excessive, we fail to obtain in an easy upright posture the beautiful simply-curved line, which we see, for instance, in the well-known picture of Nicholas Poussin, called the Arcadian Shepherds. For with excessive inclination of the pelvis the abdomen is projected forwards instead of the pelvis, and a correspondingly deep hollow is seen above the sacrum in the lumbar region of the back.

If, on the other hand, the inclination is too slight, the pelvis projects in an ungraceful fashion, and the trunk makes a conspicuous angle with the thighs. But this is a defect of less frequent occurrence. Excessive inclination of the pelvis may also mar the lower part of the back by causing the sacrum to project too much, while insufficient inclination may mar it by giving it too flat an appearance.

The typical antique iliac line in male figures, on the first impression, suggests to us that we have before us a pelvis of slight inclination, with the iliac crest bent unusually far inwards. The whole bearing of the figure, as a rule, implies a very small degree of pelvic inclination. If, further, the inward projecting angle of the iliac line is caused by the anterior superior iliac spine, as we are at once led to assume, then the whole wing of the osilium must be directed less downwards and outwards than among us, and more upwards and inwards; we have, however, no actual proof that in those times the human pelvis ever had a shape so different from that of the present time, much less that it was the prevalent form.

Among the bones of men belonging to ancient times which I have had an opportunity of investigating, I have not met with a single osilium giving evidence of such a structure, though it is true I have examined no Greek bones, but only those of Italic origin. Among the skeletons of the Felsinea Necropolis one only exhibited a somewhat more marked curve forwards and inwards of the iliac crest; but it was not so marked as would be implied by the antique type, if the above interpretation were correct. I have also found a more pronounced inward curve than is now normal in a female Egyptian mummy at Parma, but it was not present in an adjacent male mummy. The fact that in the anatomical figure by Cigoli, in the Bargello at Florence, the anterior superior iliac spine is more turned inwards than usual, and thus approximates to the antique type, does not assist us. We are bound, therefore, to entertain the possibility that the bend in the iliac line may not indicate the anterior superior iliac spine, and that the latter may lie to the inside of it, somewhere in the soft parts of the abdominal wall.

On this supposition let us try to determine its exact position as nearly as possible.

Four great muscles lie in the abdominal wall: the

rectus (Fig. 18, 1, and Fig. 19, 7), the external oblique (Fig. 18, 2), the internal oblique (Fig. 18, 3), and the transversalis abdominis muscle (Fig. 19, 4).

The rectus muscle is enclosed in a fibrous sheath composed of fibres belonging to the tendinous portion of the oblique and transversalis muscles.

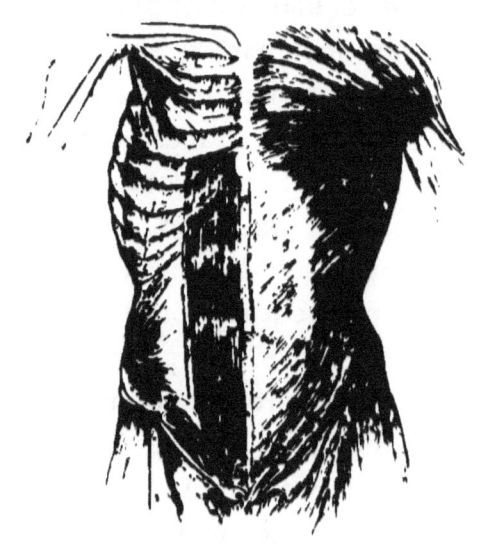

FIG. 18.

Tendinous fibres of the internal oblique muscle, and likewise tendinous fibres of the transversalis, though only to a certain depth, contribute to the hinder wall of the sheath. Nearly on a level with the anterior part of the iliac crest is a spot*

* The point marked 6 in Fig. 19 is made visible by the removal of all the left rectus muscle up to where it is situated, while the rest is seen in section. It is only necessary to follow the divided surface of the muscle in an outward direction until the point is

(Fig. 19, 6) at which all these fibres leave the hinder wall of the sheath and pass into the anterior wall, so that from this point downwards the muscle is only separated from the body cavity by a connective tissue layer, independent of the muscles, the so-called fascia

FIG. 19.

transversalis, and by the peritonæal membrane. The reached where the above-described change, in the course of the tendinous fibres, takes place. The right rectus muscle is retained in its entire length, and is seen in profile in Fig. 19, 7, and in front view in Fig. 18, 1. The left rectus is, in the latter figure, covered by the anterior wall of the sheath in which it lies. Fig. 18, 5, indicates the pyramidal muscle, which has been mentioned above in the description of the abdomen, as the muscle which, by its contraction, stretches the *linea alba.*

The illustrations are copied from those of the abdominal muscles given by L. Hollstein, in his "Anatomie des Menschen" (Berlin, 1885).

bend in the typical antique iliac line lies about on
a level with this point. Is it possible that this
change in the course of the fibres could, in a race
with powerful muscles, unfettered by close-fitting
clothing, have affected the surface of the body
much more than with us?

There is, however, yet another possibility to be
considered. The rectus muscle has three tendinous
bands (*Inscriptiones tendineæ*). Occasionally a fourth
is present, which lies midway between the umbilicus
and the symphysis pubis, and, as a rule, is only
visible in the outer part of the muscle. As this
band still occurs, though only in a minority of
instances, it may have been normally present in
antiquity ; and since such bands are closely attached
to the anterior wall of the sheath of the rectus above
mentioned, it is not inconceivable that the surface
might be affected by them. By this I do not mean
that the fourth band is visible as such, since the iliac
line does not run where it lies. It is merely suggested that it exercises a more powerful tension, and
thereby causes the iliac line to prolong its horizontal
course beyond the anterior end of the iliac crest.

This view, however, is open to a serious objection,
viz., it invariably happens that, when in the antique
the outer limit of the sheath of the rectus can be
recognised, the inward projecting angle of the iliac
line does not reach up to it, but leaves a space of
some two fingers' breadth intervening.

Are we to accept one of these possibilities as the

cause of the difference between the antique and the modern iliac line, or must we believe that a blunder was committed in the very beginning of antique sculpture, and perpetuated during its entire history?

A final judgment is not rendered less difficult when we learn that the antique type of iliac line is not wholly without its exceptions.

I recollect having seen a very fine torso in the Vatican in which the iliac line did not display the typical form, but might have been faithfully copied from an existing model. The Ganymede of the Uffizi, a masterly if disagreeable specimen of naturalistic sculpture, also shows no trace of it.*
Besides these, examples are found intermediate between the two extremes.

In a few antiques we find the natural iliac line in addition to the typical line, the two being separated from one another by a slight elevation.

Thus I was unable to discover any definite solution of my doubts until I had an opportunity, through the kindness of the distinguished sculptor, Cav. Agostino Felici, in Venice, of observing a powerfully-built young man who sat to him as a model. The antique line was quite distinctly and unmistakably

---

* It is well known that the Ganymede was a mere torso when first discovered. Benvenuto Cellini supplied the head, arms, feet, pedestal, and eagle, but it has never been suggested that he made any alteration in the region of the pelvis. The absence of the typical iliac line may perhaps be attributed to the youth of the model, although present in other antique representations of figures quite as youthful.

present in him. The lateral muscle masses lay immediately on and over the iliac crest, so as to leave
a depression, not above, but below the crest. The
fleshy roll was not due merely to the fat layer, which
was by no means pronounced. By tightening the
skin upwards I could feel the iliac crest as an essential
part of the prominence. The latter extended upwards into the region of the flank, since the abdominal
muscles, which here lie under the skin and fat, are
attached to the iliac crest.

The lower border of the prominence formed the
transverse outer (lateral) branch of the antique iliac
line. It ran considerably beneath the iliac crest,
descending anteriorly less than the latter, and then
suddenly bent at an angle downwards into the inner
(medial) descending branch of the same line. Its
whole course resembled very closely that of the iliac
line of the Apollo Belvedere. On examining the apex
of the angle with the hand, I could feel the anterior
end of the iliac crest—that is to say, the anterior
superior iliac spine. Thus all doubt was removed as
to this being the cause of the angle, and similarly
there can be no doubt that in antique statues the
angle is to be referred to the same origin. The only
question remaining is whether in several antiques in
which the two angles are nearer to each other than
in the Apollo Belvedere and in our model, the
sculptors have adhered strictly to nature, or whether
in these instances they have deviated therefrom.

Afterwards, through the kindness of the sculptor

Prof. Kühne, in Vienna, I was enabled to examine a second model illustrating the antique type. This man was also a Venetian. He had formerly been a gondolier, and was no longer young; and although not exactly stout, he had a considerable layer of fat extending on the side of the body down the flanks so as to overhang the iliac crest, and causing the transverse branch of the typical iliac line to run in a less slanting and more horizontal direction even than in the preceding model. Variations in this respect are likewise met with in the antique, and the course of the transverse branch of the line in question is dependent not only on the form and position of the pelvis, but also in the fat layer, in so far as the latter affects the elevation or depression respectively of the surface.

In no case, however, must we be led into regarding the transverse branch of this line, in antique statues, as indicating the site of the iliac crest itself, but only as a depression below the latter. The iliac crest constitutes the bony basis of the lower part of the prominence, which, owing to the softness of its upper portion, is called the fleshy ridge or roll.

From the foregoing we can now recognise the two factors which practically determine the course of the horizontal branch of the iliac line.

The first factor, the shape of the pelvis being taken as constant, is its inclination, since it is evident that this branch will run less horizontally in proportion as the inclination of the pelvis increases; and the second factor is the amount and distribution of the fat on the flanks. The branch has its fixed point of origin at the anterior superior iliac spine; it does not, however, thenceforth follow the iliac crest, but runs below it; and, other circumstances being equal, the thicker the layer of fat over the external oblique muscles and the iliac crest, the lower does the branch run, and therefore the more horizontal it is; and the fat, by its tendency to hang downwards, causes the roll to pass over into a hollow groove later, i.e., further downwards than is the case in leaner individuals.

It is hardly necessary to say that the form of the pelvis, and of the alæ of the iliac bones more especially, exercises some influence, but this may vary in so many ways and by such fine gradations as to render it impossible to lay down any general statement on the subject. To follow it out in detail would only be possible by first examining the living model and then investigating preparations of the pelvis in the dead subject.

On the last-named of the two models I made some measurements which present certain features of interest. The greatest transverse diameter of the upper pelvic region, including the fleshy masses lying above the alæ of the iliac bones, amounted to 322 millimetres. This was about 17 mm. less than the greatest diameter in the region of the hip-joint, since the latter amounted to 339 mm. The distance between the two angles so often referred to was 250 mm., and the greatest transverse diameter, measured in the depth of the furrow of the horizontal branch of the typical iliac line, amounted to 318 mm. The furrow was thus overhung by the fleshy roll above it to the extent of 2 mm. only on either side ; a fact, however, which does not prevent the line from being traced with absolute certainty, as it was defined with sufficient clearness.

The straight horizontal furrow or step, frequently seen to be sharply marked on antique male statues between the abdomen and pubic prominence, and uniting the descending branches of the two iliac lines, has originated in the sculptural representation of the upper edge of the pubic hair. Its origin may still be recognised in several statues; for instance, in the Harmodius at Naples, the Choiseul-Gouffier Apollo in the British Museum, the Doryphoros of Polycletus at Naples, the Farnese Diadumenos in London,* and others.

Its origin makes clear to us further why the line is in many figures produced so far towards the thigh as to interrupt the natural connection of the descending branch of the iliac line with the furrow between the scrotum and thigh.

The ancients appear to depart in this matter still further from nature, but they encountered the difficulty that the artist had to represent a feature not naturally adapted for sculpture, and yet one that could not be passed over.

* All these statues are figured in Sybel's "Weltgeschichte der Kunst."

9

There is, however, another mode in which the descending branch of the iliac line and the furrow between scrotum and thigh may be disunited, which is quite consonant with nature. In statues in which the weight of the body is thrown on one leg while the other is free, the disconnection is frequently seen above the supporting leg, though absent, or, at any rate, less distinct, above the other. The pelvis lies in a slanting position, and its lower portion presses more heavily on the thigh of the supporting leg than when the weight is equally distributed on both legs. In this way a cushion projects on that side, appearing as a lateral elevation of the pubic prominence, and the descending branch of the iliac line passes above it in an inward direction towards the median line, while the furrow between the thigh and scrotum in passing upwards remains below the cushion, and turning outwards is prolonged into the line which arises as a fold of the flexure between the trunk and the thigh when the thigh and knee are raised to a position at right angles to the body.

This is very clearly seen in the Discobolus who stands upright holding the quoit in his left hand, which hangs at his side, while he bends his right arm at the elbow, and gesticulates with the hand and fingers, as if he would utter some remark concerning the cast about to be made. The famous Hermes from Olympia with the infant Dionysos exhibits the same feature.

When the interruption above described is distinct on both sides, the descending branches of the typical iliac line are usually united by a line passing between the abdomen and the pubic prominence, and having the form of a curve convex below.

Obviously the most important question for us from a practical point of view is this : Ought the artist to reproduce in his works the antique typical form of iliac line or not?

There can be no question as to the excellent effect which the line produces. Even at a distance it gives proportion to the figure, and helps to diminish the superficial area of the abdomen. It gives an air of solidity ; and when we see it in the living model, there is no denying that it enhances considerably the impression of force and manly beauty. It is undoubtedly within the artist's right to impart to his work a feature which he regards as of the highest beauty, even if he has only seen it in a single instance, or has only a single unimpeachable proof of its occurrence ; but he is scarcely justified in giving form to a feature the very existence of which in the present or in the past is a matter of doubt.

Our artists are fully entitled to make the second toe of the foot longer than the great toe, since, though not the rule in the existing race of men, it does occur, not only in children, but likewise in adults, and moreover in adults of the Aryan stock, as I shall show further on ; in many antiques, however, we find the iliac line with the inward angles brought curiously near to each other, and so deeply and ruggedly defined that the modern artist cannot but hesitate about reproducing it until it is forthcoming in a living example. He should, however, seek for models who show an approximation to the antique type, and avoid reproducing an abdomen such as was possessed by the model who served Rembrandt for his Christ before Pilate.

The artists of the renaissance and of modern times have varied in their practice, adopting sometimes the antique type, and sometimes the form now prevalent in nature. A striking example of the former is seen in the Perseus of Benvenuto Cellini, in the Loggia dei Lanzi at Florence, and in the Mars of Sansovino, on the staircase of the Ducal Palace at Venice. In the instance just named the artist has misunderstood his antique pattern, as he has prolonged the line running from the hips horizontally as far as the sheath of the recti muscles.

We also find the antique form of line in drawings attributed to Raffaelle. Later the artists adhered rather to the modern type which they observed in their models. Thus I do not remember ever to have seen an instance of the antique type in the nude male figures of Guido Reni.

In a drawing in the Uffizi (No. 2), ascribed to Andrea del Verocchio, both lines, the realistic and the antique, are present together, and the same thing also occurs elsewhere, and occasionally passes over into the type in which the descending branches of the typical form unite into an arch carved below, and lying between the abdomen and the pubic prominence, while the line between the pubes and the thigh merges into the flexure of the thigh, and so follows a course below the iliac line and quite distinct from it.

If we inquire why the typical iliac line is not

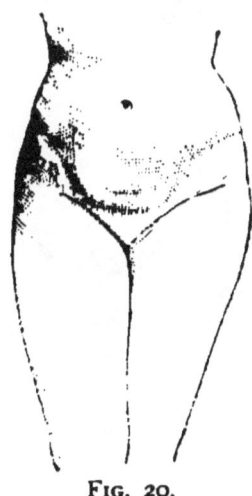

FIG. 20.

present in an antique female figure, the answer is that the form of pelvis which really gives rise to the typical line, and is indispensable to its production, is extremely rare in the female.

In the female pelvis the alæ of the iliac bones are generally less perpendicular and curved inwards than in the male ; they slant outwards more, and thus the distance between the two anterior superior iliac spines is increased. To this last-named feature it is mainly due that the presence of the line which we see in antique male figures becomes impossible in the female.

I have, nevertheless, once observed a very marked indication of it in a photograph from the life, from which the accompanying woodcut (Fig. 20) is copied. It was quite possible, in the distribution of light and shade, to recognise the point corresponding to the angle in antique male statues, and from it to trace the typical line more or less distinctly downwards

Fig. 21.

and outwards; but owing to the greater width of the pelvis relatively to its height, the angle is more obtuse, and the descending rami of the typical line are less perpendicular. When this is taken into consideration, such indications are traceable in antique female figures more or less distinctly; for instance, in the three famous statues of Venus, that of Milo, the Capitoline, and the Medicean.

Fig. 21, which is also reproduced from a photograph of the living model, exhibits this line, and likewise forms approaching the male type.

In the female we may distinguish two extreme
types, which, at first sight, are difficult to reconcile.
In the first, the inguinal line, that is, the line
separating the thighs from the pubic prominence
and the lowest part of the abdomen, ascends, as in
most living men, direct to the anterior superior iliac
spine.

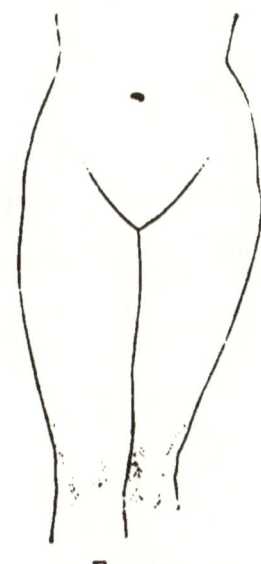

FIG. 22.

The characteristic feature of the second type is
that the inguinal line pursues a different course from
that of the iliac line, bending outwards, and being
traceable at some distance below the anterior superior
iliac spine as a transverse line separating the trunk
from the thighs. It becomes a line of the flexure
of the thighs; and though it may disappear or be
very slightly marked when the leg is kept quite

straight, it may become conspicuous, if the thigh is flexed a very little, as, for instance, in walking, as is seen in the female figure of a group in marble belonging to the Marchese Nicolini, in the vestibule on the first floor of the Bargello at Florence.

Fig. 22 illustrates the first type, Fig. 23 the second. These two types are, however, connected

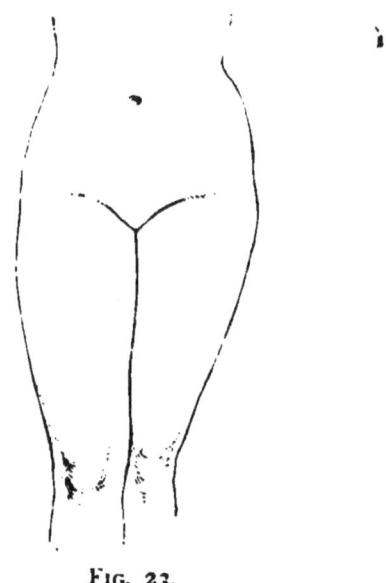

FIG. 23.

by an intermediate form, in which the two lines are equally conspicuous. According as the one or the other is more pronounced, the figure approximates to the first or second type.

When both lines are present and completely separate, they generally take the following course : the iliac line proper starts from the anterior end of the iliac crest, which either projects, as is the case in lean persons, or is concealed by the tissues lying over it. The line does not commence as a fold, but as a slight depression ; follows in the main the direction of the femoral arch (*Arcus inguinalis*, also called Fallopius', or, less correctly, Poupart's ligament, a tendinous line running on either side from the anterior superior iliac spine to the anterior ends of the pubic bones, where they meet in the pubic prominence) ; bends with a curve inwards, and unites with that of the opposite side at the boundary of the abdomen and the pubic prominence.

Occasionally we also see a depression running from the starting-point of our line in a horizontal direction outwards, and forming an obtuse angle with it. It thus corresponds with the angular bend, which, however, comes nearer to a right angle, in the iliac line of the antique male figure. Instances of its occurrence were given above in Figs. 20 and 21.

The second line is that which has just been described. It arises at the inner side of the thigh, ascends in a diagonal direction between the thigh and the pubic prominence, and then bends outward in a transverse direction, thus dividing the thigh from the whole of the trunk rather than from the abdomen only. The distinct development of this part of the line, and its controlling influence on the distribution of the proportions of the whole figure, characterize the less frequent type, one, however, which largely contributes to the beauty of many works of antiquity and the renaissance. The main characteristic of the ordinary type consists in the external portion of the second line being marked either very faintly or not at all, and in the line which ascends between the pubes and the thigh passing over more or less distinctly into the depression which descends from the anterior superior iliac spine, or at any rate running more or less closely to it instead of tending to diverge from it.

The form which these lines take is, in a great degree, dependent on the attitude of the body; so much so that in one and the same figure one side may apparently * approximate to the extreme form of one type, and the other side to the other type, as may be seen from the accompanying woodcut (Fig. 24). It is reproduced from the photograph of a girl carrying a vessel on her head, and supporting it with the right hand. But the attitude is not the sole element. Two persons standing in exactly the same attitude will exhibit differences, which are the result of variations in the distribution of the fatty tissue, and also in the form of the pelvis. The course taken by these lines is further closely connected with the obliquity of the pelvis, and with the direction of the neck of the femur, since it is evident that if the latter

* "Apparently," because a careful examination of the figure will show that on the left side the line of the flexure of the thigh does not ascend to the anterior superior iliac spine, but to a point situated at nearly three fingers' breadth distance below and outside it.

is directed much upwards, the trochanter will come to lie more below the line about which the thigh-bones rotate when flexed on the trunk, than if the neck of the femur lies in a horizontal position. This line passes, in fact, through the centre of the head of the femur.

In several very beautiful figures bequeathed to us

Fig. 24.

by antiquity and the renaissance, the lines of the flexure of the thighs meet at a very obtuse angle; and, owing to the iliac line proper being invisible, form the principal lines of distribution of the figure, in which the thighs are then marked off from the whole trunk rather than merely from the abdomen.

The ancients have also left us a series of statues in which the thighs are only divided off from the pubic prominence, or but very little further, by a

definite and easily-traced line, while the remainder
of the border region between the trunk and the
thighs presents a soft fleshy surface.   The renaissance
also produced similar figures, though usually more
distinct demarcations were preferred.   In ancient
times people sat less often, while they lay down and
stood upright more than in later times.

It depends on circumstances whether a distinct
demarcation or an even surface of transition should
be preferred.   The first may be preferable particularly
in monumental and ornamental figures calculated to
be viewed from a distance, while the latter may
rather be selected where the distance is less, and a
form of beauty is aimed at which the spectator shall
realize for himself in flesh and blood.

It should be added that it is possible for three
furrows to be seen on the hips, one above the other,
shallow indeed and indistinct, so as to be visible only
in a favourable light.   They are to be found, for
instance, above the free leg of the Capitoline Venus.
The lowest one forms the border-line between the
thigh and the mons veneris, and marks off the thigh,
which is slightly advanced from the body, or rather
from the hip.   The second lies on a level with the
depression between abdomen and mons ; and the
third and last runs from the site of the anterior
superior iliac spine outwards, and corresponds
anatomically to the horizontal branch of the typical
iliac line of antique male statues.

Now let us consider a little more in detail the

inclination of the pelvis, and its influence on the
general appearance of the figure. The woodcut
below (Fig. 25) represents a human pelvis as seen in
profile, on which three lines are drawn, meeting in
the axis of rotation of the acetabulum ; one is a line
of dashes, the second a continuous line, and the third
dotted. Let us first take the continuous line, and

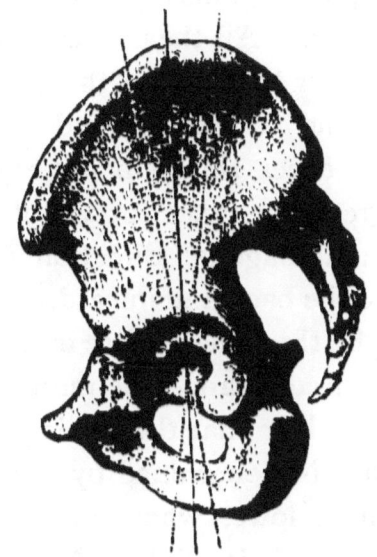

FIG. 25.

afterwards the dotted line, as being vertical ; then it
is evident that the inclination of the pelvis is greater
in the latter case, and it is further evident that all
points on the pelvis situated below the point of
rotation are then shifted backwards, the lowest points
being shifted the furthest backwards. If we next
take the line of dashes as the vertical line, the
inclination is less, and all points on the pelvis below

the point of rotation are shifted forwards, the lowest being shifted furthest. Thus, when the inclination is marked, these points all lie further backwards; and more forwards when it is slight.

Now all the muscles lying on the inside of the femur, except the sartorius, take their origin, so far as they have a pelvic origin, in a line beginning at the upper end of the symphysis pubis and ending at the tuberosity of the ischium. All these muscular attachments, therefore, lie further back when the pelvic inclination is considerable, and further forward when it is slight. It follows that, other things being equal, when the inclination is great, the inner surface of the thigh will be flattened in a diagonal direction from the front and outwards to the back and inwards. Where the inclination is slight, the same surface in its upper portion will, under like circumstances, be more rounded.

Likewise it is clear that the pubic prominence, the position of which is determined by that of the pubic symphysis, will be lower when the pelvic inclination is great than when it is slight. Now' since the iliac line, which descends from the anterior end of the iliac crest, runs down between the pubic prominence and the thigh, the thighs, if their surfaces are flattened away inwards from the front, leave a wedge-shaped space enclosing the pubic prominence, which is drawn down between them.

The effect is different when the inclination of the pelvis is inconsiderable, especially if the inside of the femur is furnished with a good cushion of fat. Such thighs, when the pelvis is not over-broad, and when the neck of the femur does not lie too much in a horizontal position, close up completely almost at the surface, without leaving a deep interval, as in the case of strong inclination.

I regard the second type as preferable, since the figures which exhibit it are, in general, better adapted for reproduction than those of the former type. They have better shaped thighs, and a more completely closed junction of the thighs; they do not thrust the abdomen forwards in standing and walking, and present a better contour of the entire figure, not only in front, but from the side also. The thighs, however, if a side view is desired, must be powerful, as their antero-posterior diameter is smaller than it would be if the pelvic inclination were considerable, because the ischial bones lie more to the front. If we seek for examples of pelvic inclination in art, the Eve, in the Loggie of the Vatican, who is picking the forbidden fruit for Adam, presents a degree of inclination that ought not to be exceeded. An equally marked inclination may be ascribed to the Eve in subsequent Expulsion from Paradise, but cannot be so accurately determined on account of the forward movement of the figure.

An example of the smallest allowable degree of inclination is furnished by the Three Graces in the Opera del Duomo at Siena (formerly in the sacristy of the Cathedral), especially in that one who is turning her back to us in Lombardi's photograph

and also in the one standing to the right hand of
the latter.

The ancients were, in general, not fond of a strong
inclination of the pelvis, either in the male or the
female, for they have seldom given it a place in ideal
art. With regard to the angle at which the lines
separating the thighs from the pubes meet, great
variety prevails among them. In the Three Graces
above mentioned it is very obtuse, far exceeding a
right angle. In the Venus, No. 134 in the Uffizi,
who is girding on the sword of Mars, and has a vase
covered with a cloth at her side, it is considerably
larger than in the Venus de Medicis. It is less than
a right angle in the Esquiline Venus in the Museum
of the Capitol. The latter is the realistic figure of a
well-formed vigorous girl, still young and of faultless
proportions, though the head is rather large in comparison with other antique sculptures, which leads
one to infer that the original was not above middle
height.

When the ilio-femoral ligament is long,—and, the
shape of the pelvis being constant, a long ligament
causes the pelvic inclination to be slight,*—it has a

* I am speaking here of the anatomical or true inclination of the
pelvis, as measured by the angle which the axis of the pelvis
makes with the plane of the thigh-bones when the ilio-femoral
ligaments are stretched. It should be distinguished, not only
from the occasional, but also from the habitual pelvic inclination.
Many persons only extend their thigh-bones so as to stretch
the ilio-femoral ligament quite exceptionally, and are in the
habit of standing with the pelvis more inclined than it is in

favourable effect on the gait. If the ligament is short, the natural inclination of the pelvis, as we have seen, is strong. If then the stride in walking has to be made at all considerable, the position of the hinder leg creates momentarily a still stronger obliquity. The centre of gravity of the trunk must not be shifted forwards beyond a definite point, dependent on the rapidity of the movement, as otherwise the body would overbalance in a forward direction. The increased inclination cannot, therefore, be attained merely by bending the entire trunk forwards ; the spinal column in the lumbar region must also be more strongly curved, and this is rendered difficult since the said curve is usually in itself—that is, in standing at ease—considerable in cases of strong pelvic inclination. These conditions are the cause of excessive inclination being so often associated with a gait that, while in no way conducing to speed, is in persons of a quick temperament often hasty and ungraceful. I remark that the association often occurs, as the gait cannot be judged without taking the

the strict anatomical sense. Again, in the regulation attitude of the body required of the German soldier, the ilio-femoral ligament is not stretched, as has already been observed by Hans Virchow. We must always bear in mind that there are two positions in which the trunk may be poised on the thighs with a minimum of muscular effort: one is that in which the ilio-femoral ligament is stretched; the other, that in which the centre of gravity of the trunk is directly supported, so that its tendency to fall is both equal and at a minimum on every side. In the former case the tendency to fall is greatest in a backward direction, but is restrained by the stretched ligament.

flexibility of the lumbar region of the spinal cord into consideration, and also the length of the legs, which regulates, according to the laws of the pendulum, the pace of the gait in which forward movement is made with the least exertion.

The women of the Romagna, especially those belonging to certain districts in the Sabine mountains, owe the regal bearing which distinguishes them so remarkably not only to their habit of carrying light loads on their heads, often without any support from their hands, but materially also to the favourable build and proportions of their bodies. This is shown by the superiority of their gait over that of women of other races who have the same habits. I do not dispute the beneficial effect of their habit, for I have remarked that, where it prevails, the gait and bearing are better than where burdens, according as they are light or heavy, are borne on the arm or back respectively.[*]

Broad hips are regarded by the general public as

---

[*] G. B. Duchenne, of Boulogne, in his " Physiologie des Mouvements " (Paris, 1867), p. 733 (German edition by C. Wernicke, Cassel and Berlin, 1885, p. 580) makes the following statement : " I believe that an inclination of the pelvis of 63 to 64 degrees, and a corresponding curvature of the lumbo-sacral region of the spinal column, are the most usual.

" I do not mean to assert that this degree of curvature should be enjoined on Art as something absolute, as a rule governing the most beautiful forms, since it has been proved that the physiological saddle-formation " (which only occurs in cases of strong pelvic inclination, as the saddle is, as a matter of fact, formed by the dorsal side of the strongly-inclined pelvis) "is ugly in men and as becoming in women. The latter judgment, however, is not the outcome of a study of the nude, but is the result of a fashion in dress, which at various times has led to pinching in the waist, and so causing the width of the hips below it to become as prominent as possible.

Nevertheless, this habit has induced many artists, both in the present and in past time, to endow their figures with abnormally broad hips. Bodies, however, resembling a violin in general outline, such as we occasionally see, especially towards the close of the middle ages and in the early renaissance in Germany, are in truth very ugly. The width of the hips in a woman must always bear a certain relative proportion to three other dimensions, viz., to the height of the whole figure, to the breadth of the shoulders, and to the smallest transverse diameter of the trunk, which is to be found between the iliac crests and the ribs.

If we imagine the Venus de Medicis standing up-

one of the distinguishing characters of many races, being a hereditary peculiarity in certain families and in certain places, and one with which the artist has to reckon, since it is rightly regarded as a feature contributing in an especial degree to the beauty of the lines of the body, more particularly in women. Besides, ancient art would enter a protest against such a rule being laid down as absolute, for we meet with very beautiful types of saddle-formation in some statues—indeed, they were much sought after by the Greeks. It is from this characteristic feature of beauty that the Venus Callipygos derives her name."

As far as this last statement is concerned, it is difficult to form any judgment of the pelvic obliquity and degree of curvature of right, as Schadow has drawn her in his "Polycletus," then, taking 100 as the height of the whole figure, the three above-mentioned dimensions will, according to the drawing in that work, have the following values : the breadth of the shoulders will be equal to 25, the least transverse diameter of the trunk to 15·4, the breadth of the hips to 20·5.

the spinal column which the Venus would possess in an erect attitude.   The difficulty arises from the unusual position in which the figure is placed.   Moreover, I do not think that the supreme artistic finish of the work, which is said to have made Canova decline the task of restoring the statue, justifies us in regarding it as a representative work of genuine classical Greek art.

I do not willingly enter the lists against one like Duchenne, who has done so much to promote the good of mankind and of science; but I ought to call the reader's attention to two points :—

1. When Duchenne speaks of the inclination of the pelvis, he refers to the ordinary inclination—that which is present when the individual is standing upright ; but I refer to the anatomical inclination, which depends on the amount of play allowed by the ilio-femoral ligament, and therefore on the length of the latter, by which the inclination is eventually determined.   It is the minimum of inclination, which is attained when the individual, standing with the legs straight and close together and the feet touching one another, holds the lower part of the trunk as far forward as he can while keeping the knees rigid.   The inclination is not measured by the angle formed by the axis of the pelvis or by its conjugate diameter with the horizon, but by the angle made with these lines by the thighs when extended on the median plane of the body.   (*Cf.* Hermann Meyer, of Zürich, "Die Beckenneigung," in Reichert and Du Bois-Reymond's "Archiv für Anatomie u. Physiologie, 1861, p. 137.)

2. Duchenne brings the curvature of the spinal column into direct and necessary connection with the pelvic inclination, whereas

I have given these measurements from the drawing. It is possible, however, that a fresh examination of the original statue might yield a somewhat greater relative breadth of the hips. Still, the important fact for us is that the drawing produces a perfectly satisfactory effect, not by any means that of a figure too narrow at the hips.

the connection, though it undoubtedly exists, has a relative character only. The spinal column may be curved when the pelvis is very slightly inclined, if the head is inclined forwards, and still more so if it happens at the same time that large heavy female breasts have to be counterbalanced. To effect this the shoulders must be held far enough back to restore equilibrium. On the other hand, a pelvis only slightly inclined anatomically in the sense above defined by me may, with a sufficient degree of flexibility in the spinal column, be placed at will in a position of increased inclination, so as to give an appearance of greater curvature to the lumbar region of the spinal column in the upright position.

Duchenne praises highly the flexibility of the spinal column and the curvature of the lumbar region in its connection with the sacrum,—the saddle-formation, as he calls it, exhibited by the Spanish women, and especially by the natives of Andalusia. He says (*loc. cit.*, p. 728 ; German edition, p. 575): "I have seen Spanish ladies in whom the lumbar curvature and its flexibility were so remarkable that they could bend the body backwards until they touched the ground with their heads."

This power depends mainly on the flexibility of the spinal column and on the activity of the extensor muscles, and also on the form of the thoracic portion of the spinal column. It is favoured by a thoracic spinal column which is but slightly convex behind and concave in front. The feat in question appears, from representations that have come down to us, to have been performed by female acrobats in ancient times. It is more easily executed when the pelvic inclination is slight than when it is

I will further add that in well-built women the greatest breadth of the hips is never above the trochanters, but either on a level with them, or, even better, below them. I say "better below the trochanters," because, if in a figure resting on both feet the outline of the thighs does not bulge at all below the trochanters, but, on the contrary, the transverse diameter at once diminishes as soon as the weight of the figure is thrown on one leg only, an ugly flattening is observable on the outside of the

pronounced, since the greater the amount of play allowed by the ilio-femoral ligament for a backward flexion of the body on the thighs, the less does the spinal column require to be curved in the lumbar region.

Flexibility of the spinal column is assuredly, under any circumstances, an advantage to the figure, but it is independent of the length of the ilio-femoral ligament, depending rather on the constitution of the vertebræ, of the intervertebral discs, and of the ligaments; also on the character of the thorax, the degree of rigidity of its component parts, and the resistance they offer to the movements of the spinal column. If a child six months old be laid on its stomach with its head raised and supported on its arms, the thoracic portion of its spinal column will become concave to a degree quite impossible in an adult.

Any one who studies the antique without prejudice will agree with me that the Greek sculptors did not favour marked pelvic inclination, either in the male or the female, though a few instances are to be found. Of the latter there are not so many as occur among the figures of the full renaissance period. On the other hand, if we examine the countless beautiful figures represented in profile on reliefs and vases with the breast and shoulders sloping backwards, and the head and pelvis inclined forwards, the lines we here meet with are wholly incompatible with a strong anatomical inclination of the pelvis.

thigh, while the trochanter of the same leg forms an angular projection. This is a defect to which I shall refer more in detail further on.

The figure of a woman with broad hips is shown to considerable disadvantage when represented in a recumbent position, resting on one trochanter. The other one then becomes very prominent, and the outline falls sharply down towards the waist, forming a disagreeable line, especially if the upper part of the body is supported on the elbow, and the spinal column is curved laterally in consequence in the lumbar region. Unfortunately modern art offers numerous examples of these unpleasing figures.

Some artists have thought it necessary to furnish their figures of Eve with unusually broad hips, wishing thereby to indicate the characteristic of maternity in the mother of the human race. A moderate breadth of the hips is, however, in the eyes of the medical man, adequate to any degree of fruitfulness. The dimension of the pelvis, which most frequently by its restricted size offers serious obstacles in childbirth, is not the transverse diameter, the extent of which is determined by the distance of the two acetabula from one another, but the diameter measured from the upper end of the sacrum to the pubic symphysis. Moreover, the breadth of the hips is not exclusively dependent on the distance between the acetabula, but also on the length of the neck of the femur, and the degree in which its direction deviates from the horizontal.

Models who have an excessive breadth of the hips have a complete closure at the junction of the thighs with the pubes only when the thighs are thick and well-rounded ; if they are somewhat thin, and, at the same time, the inclination of the pelvis is at all pronounced, the closure above indicated is very imperfect, and this constitutes one of the most disagreeable defects to which a female model is liable.

VII.

A S in the hip-joint, so also in the knee-joint, there is a ligament which prevents over-extension, and enables us, without any special muscular effort, to maintain the thigh in an upright position on the leg. This is the anterior crucial ligament of the knee-joint (*Ligamentum cruciatum anterius*).

On the upper articular surface of the tibia may be seen in the centre an eminence (*Eminentia inter-condyloidea tibiæ*), and in front of it a fossa. From the latter arises a strong ligament, which, as it crosses another which arises behind the eminence, is called the anterior crucial ligament. The fibres of this ligament run obliquely upwards, outwards, and backwards, and are attached to the inner surface of the external condyle of the femur. When the leg is extended in a line with the thigh, this ligament is stretched tight, and prevents any further extension. The longer the ligament is, and the more play it allows to the bones, the smaller is the angle which the thigh makes with the leg in standing at ease; and the less freedom of movement the ligament allows, the more nearly does the angle become equal to two right angles, or 180°. When we consider the shape of the leg, we must start from the position in which the individual stands erect and has his toes turned straight to the front, both feet being supported along their entire length, and the anterior crucial ligament being stretched tight.

It is the same position as that in which the ilio-femoral ligament is stretched, and which formed our starting-point in determining the inclination of the pelvis, because a man, if he bends the knee while standing upright, may render its inclination to the horizon less than is natural to it.

The anterior crucial ligament of the knee-joint is never too short in models, though frequently too long. It can never be too short, because, in all normally-developed human beings, it is stretched, at an early age, sufficiently to allow of the leg being completely extended. Whether it is too long may be determined in the following manner. The model is placed in the attitude above described, and examined in profile view; a point is then found in the centre of the broadest part of the thigh, below the level where the posterior outline of the thigh passes into that of the buttock. From this central point a straight line is imagined drawn down to the outer ankle-bone (*Malleolus externus*). This line may be rendered visible by stretching a black thread on the leg between the two points mentioned. The thread then divides the thigh into an anterior and a posterior half, and ought to pass through the middle of the knee. If it lies more in front towards the patella, the anterior crucial ligament is too long in proportion, and the knee is consequently arched in a backward direction.

It may be added, however, that a slight deviation

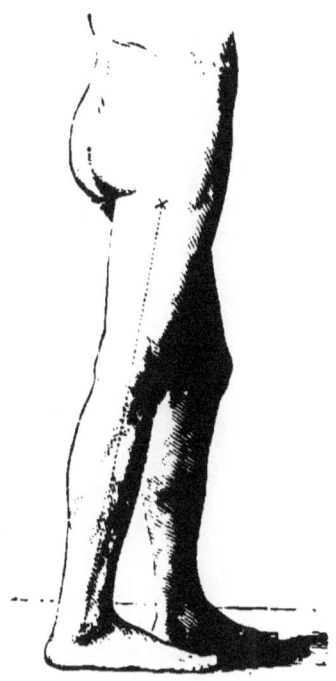

FIG. 26.

of this kind from the straight line is not, under all circumstances, objectionable, especially in powerfully-formed male legs.

In some individuals and in certain attitudes legs with the knees curved rather more backwards than would be allowable under the above rule, may give satisfactory lines. In order to demonstrate the course of the test-line above described, I have laid it down in the annexed woodcuts. Fig. 26 represents the leg of a man, Fig. 27 that of a woman; both from photographs of the living model. An objection may be raised that the two figures are not absolutely in profile, but, as a matter of fact, the leg is so. The

Fig. 27.

slightly-posterior aspect presented in each case is due to a rotation of the hip-joint.

In addition to an excessive length of the anterior crucial ligament, we meet with another defect in the leg which also becomes visible in profile view. It is apt to convey an impression that the thigh does not rest properly on the leg, the thigh being shifted too far forward, and the leg standing too far back. The defect is associated with slight inclination of the pelvis and a strongly-developed muscular system, and thigh-bones that have their convex surfaces turned towards the front. The effect of the latter is obvious.; while the muscles assist through the strong bulging caused by the extensor of the knee-joint on the one hand and the muscles of the calf on the other. The slightness of the pelvic inclination affects the result in so far as it causes the posterior outline of the thigh to become less prominent, as compared with that of the calf, than where the inclination is pronounced. Such legs do not produce a good effect ; though in men of a compact and vigorous build they may be character-istic. Next let us examine the leg in its anterior aspect.

It is generally accepted that when a man stands erect with legs and feet close together, the two legs should be in contact at four points : viz., (1)' at the upper part of the thigh ; (2) between the knees, or, more accurately, between the inner condyles of the two thigh-bones ; (3) at the point where the two calves bulge furthest inwards ; (4) at the inner ankle-bones.

Schadow, in his " Polycletus," has drawn in this way all the figures in that attitude. And the rule may be regarded as correct, especially in the female, with this addition, that where the lower limbs are powerful and somewhat inclined to fatness, the thighs may be in contact along the whole or nearly the whole of their length without its being regarded as

a defect. Indeed, it is not unlikely that this would
be the case with the Venus de Medicis if she came
to life. It is true that Schadow, who from careful
measurements has drawn her in an erect position, has
not so represented her ; but the lower part of the
thigh in his drawing looks to me more slender than
in the original. It is certainly to be considered a
defect if, when the ankles are touching, the knees
cannot be completely extended without a pressure or
friction arising between the condyles of the thigh-
bones. The corresponding points of the two legs
should meet without pressure, and the one condyle
should not knock against the other. When this
takes place, it is because the knee is too much curved
inwards, and we have already, though only in a
commencing stage, to deal with the knock-kneed
condition. The very frequent occurrence of this
defect in female models should put the artist on his
guard, nor should he suffer himself to be misled by
the fact that some celebrated female figures have the
knee curved inwards. For example, it occurs in
the Venus de Medicis, but is there due merely to the
position of the free leg, which is somewhat bent at
the knee ; if the supporting leg is examined, it will
be found to be straight. Legs defective in this
respect occur, not only in women, but also in figures
of angels, doubtless in consequence of female models
being used so often by artists for their angels.

The opposite deviation from the norm, if at all
considerable, is very ugly in female figures, and is

the more conspicuous because it rarely occurs in nature. A very small amount of deviation in this direction, leaving, however, the whole leg perfectly straight, may be scarcely noticed. The Three Graces in the Opera del Duomo at Siena are certainly some of the noblest among the youthful female figures bequeathed to us by the ancients; and yet, if that one who in Lombardi's photograph turns her back to us, and who is headless and almost armless, is carefully examined, it may be doubted whether the knees would touch if the feet were brought close together.

In the male model juxtaposition of the knees is less of a desideratum than in the female. It is true there ought to be no large space between them, as in a bow-legged individual; on the other hand, it is not necessary that there should be actual contact. And the same holds good with respect to contact between the calves. We may as well draw attention to a couple of test-lines which help us to judge, not only of any leg in the living subject, but likewise of any leg of a statue which supports the body in an erect position with the toes turned to the front. They are two straight lines, which meet at the highest point of the instep. One starts from the median line of the body at the level of the pubes, the other from the point of the external contour of the thigh, where the great trochanter lies close under the skin. Now when the legs are close together, the knees may lie so far apart as to allow of the patella falling exactly between these two lines, but no further.

In the art of the renaissance, even of the early renaissance, we meet with some instances of a still more curved type of leg; but I do not think they ought to be regarded as worthy of imitation. The German renaissance occasionally furnishes examples of figures that come near to being bow-legged. Quite recently they have been reproduced in ornamental figures on objects made in the style of the German renaissance, in order to be "true to the style."

Legs so made "true to the style" generally err in two respects : firstly, the knee is bent too far backwards, as if the anterior crucial ligament were too long ; and, in the second place, the knee is curved outwards more than it should be.

Sometimes, however, the latter error is avoided, and yet the leg looks wrong in a front view, which is due to its being modelled as if the upper part of the tibia were concave on the inside to a degree which, as a matter of fact, does occur in nature, though it is neither beautiful nor normal.

But this type of leg does not produce so disagreeable an effect in male figures as that in which both knees are curved inwards and backwards. These are the worst of all, and any model owning them should be discarded. It was perhaps scarcely needful to call attention to their ugliness. Notwithstanding, the decorative art of the last century includes figures of Hercules which exhibit them in a way that almost deserves to be called shameless.

The knock-kneed condition of the legs, so prevalent

in women, also occasions a disfigurement of the knees when bent. This defect is due to an inequality in the height of the two condyles of the femur.

If the femur in a skeleton be placed on the top of the tibia, so that the surfaces of the joints are in contact, the two bones will not lie in a straight line, but make an obtuse angle externally, which becomes more acute in proportion as the individual was knock-kneed during life. When such a knock-kneed leg is flexed, the internal condyle of the femur projects more prominently than in a normal leg, and the furrow between the two condyles which determines the position of the patella is directed more outwards and less to the front than in legs that are straight. The consequence is, that in the bent knee the patella faces more outwards, and thus causes a disfigurement, which increases proportionately if the patella is large and prominent, while, as mentioned above, a second ugly prominence appears on the inner side, occasioned by the internal condyle of the femur.

Many models acquire a peculiarly ungraceful appearance when, as usual in standing figures, they are placed in such an attitude that the body is supported mainly on one leg, leaving the other free, the latter affording but little support, so that almost the entire weight of the body is poised on the one leg only. This causes the external contour of the latter to lose its curve, and form a nearly straight line from the outside of the knee-joint up to the great trochanter, which then makes an ugly angular prominence.

The woodcut (Fig. 28), copied from a photograph from life, gives an illustration of this disagreeable line, though by no means in its most offensive form.

When we inquire into the cause of this deformity and examine the bones, we cannot avoid remarking that it is favoured by a long and horizontally-directed

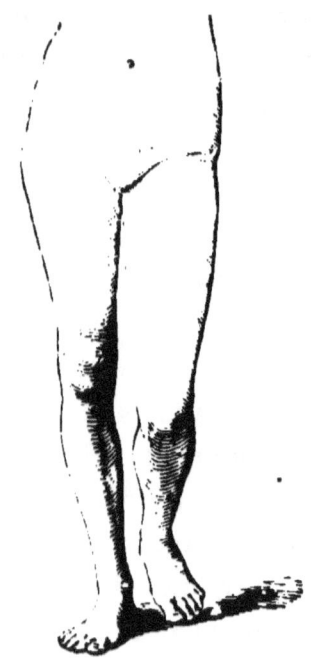

Fig. 28.

neck of the femur, which, if the pelvis is sufficiently broad between the hip-joints, makes the great trochanter jut out strongly on either side. If, moreover, the ilium has a vertical position, its upper border on the side of the supporting leg will incline inwards, because the pelvis is slanting, by reason of the supporting leg standing higher than the free leg. The consequence is, that the outline of the hip above the trochanter makes a pronounced bend inwards, and so causes the latter to become still more prominent.

The shape of the shaft of the femur may also be not without some influence. There are femora of which the middle portion, when viewed from the front, reveals a slight inward deflection, which is almost wholly absent in others.

This type of femur must yield a rather less curved outline of the thigh, since just at the point where it should be rounded by the *vastus externus* muscle, the bony foundation of the muscle retreats inwards.

In the next place, we have to consider the co-operation of the muscles. If the body is supported little or not at all on the side of the free leg, the task of maintaining the trunk upright falls, in the first place, on the *gluteus medius* and *minimus* muscles, as they extend from the outer surface of the ilium down to the great trochanter. They receive valuable assistance, however, from the *tensor fasciæ latæ*, or *tensor vaginæ femoris*, as it is also called. Through the contraction of the latter, the *fascia lata* is drawn up over the thigh, like close-fitting breeches held up by braces that are fastened too high, and so the outline of the thigh is rendered tense and straight.

Lastly, the shape of the thigh may be affected by an unfavourable distribution, or by the absence of fat.

The ugliness of this form of thigh, however, has not always availed to prevent its being imitated. At the annual exhibition of the Künstlerhaus at Vienna, in 1884, a group in plaster over life-size was shown, in which a female figure, although intended to produce an impression of beauty, was very obviously marred by this defect.

Absolute realism would justify its reproduction, since it very frequently occurs in nature ; and even in finely formed men contraction of the *tensor fasciæ latæ* renders the external outline of the thigh flat and straight.

The woodcut (Fig. 28) is faithfully copied from the photograph of an excellent academy model. But the line is sometimes so bad in its effect that it should be avoided at any cost. It is seen under its best aspect in individuals who have the centre of the femur deflected outwards rather than inwards, and in whom the trochanter does not project, provided that the muscles are well developed, and the fat so distributed on the thigh as to increase the curve of the external outline.

If this defect is present in a model, and the artist is disinclined to alter it, he should seek, if the action allow of it, to give the weight of the body more support on the side of the free leg, and so attain a more favourable configuration. In practice artists do not hesitate, as a rule, in such cases to make such corrections as their feeling suggests.

A very common defect in models, both male and female, is thickness of the knees. It is very ugly, and though often found in individuals otherwise admirably formed, the artist should not be led away into reproducing it. The Greek and Roman sculptors were careful to avoid it. Even the Farnese Hercules, certainly the heaviest figure that the ancients have bequeathed to us, has by no means thick knees.

The primary cause of thick knees is a clumsy type of skeleton, usually associated with a general thickness of the joints,—in this instance, of the condyles of the femur. Slenderness of the latter, however, does not always stand in a definite relation to that of the whole skeleton. We meet with thick thigh-bones furnished with condyles of moderate dimensions, and, on the other hand, slender thigh-bones with thick condyles. The girth of the knee may also be increased by fatty deposits, which are injurious to its shape, more particularly when they do not harmonize in amount with the fat on other parts of the body, and when they obliterate details of its structure. Celebrated masters, in working from models of a not over-lean type, have also reproduced this fat on the knees, as, for instance, the Caracci in some figures in the frescoes in the Palazzo Farnese, and Guido Reni in his soaring figures of Fortune, in which the wrists are likewise overlaid with superfluous fat, as also in other female figures of the same master.

Finally, we must not leave unnoticed the fact that constant kneeling on a hard surface ruins the knees, either by growths in the skin and subjacent cellular tissue, or by alterations in the parts belonging to the joint itself.

The knee-cap should be small and distinctly recognisable, not projecting, however, nor forming a
so-called pointed knee. No protrusion ought to be
visible beneath it, such as often results from much
kneeling ; on the contrary, the great extensor tendon
of the joint (*Ligamentum patellæ*) joining the knee-
cap to the tibia should be visible, but only when
the extensor muscles are contracted ; when they are
relaxed, the knee-cap sinks, and the extensor tendon,
being now also relaxed, is no longer perceptible
through the integument.

In the leg we are principally concerned with two
points—a pure tibial line, and a well-marked calf.

The tibia should, in general, present an even line,
not a straight one, for it is never straight ; but it
ought not to exhibit any abnormal degree of concavity, nor should its line be broken by local
prominences on the bone.

What we have called the tibial line does not, in any
action or under any aspect, owe its shape exclusively
to the bone itself. It does so most nearly when an
individual lies on his back, and the calves of the legs
face downwards with the muscles relaxed, but even
so not entirely. In the lower portion of the leg, that
nearest the foot, lie two tendons, one belonging to
the anterior muscle of the tibia (*M. tibialis anticus*),
and the other to the long extensor of the great toe
(*M. extensor hallucis longus*) ; they lie nearer to the
skin than the tibia itself, and so carry on the outline
in the lower part of its course. In the erect position

the fleshy belly of the *tibialis anticus* muscle also projects beyond the tibia in the leg supporting the weight of the body, and so alters the aspect of the skin in profile. This bulging, which is especially marked in vigorously-developed male legs, cannot be neglected, but it is none the less difficult to handle successfully, since, if it projects too much, the leg easily acquires a thick, club-shaped form, owing to the muscles of the calf also bulging out behind.

The prominence of the *tibialis anticus* muscle is most pronounced in active dorsal flexion—that is, when the foot and the points of the toes are directed upwards and the heel downwards; it disappears, on the other hand, when the toes are extended downwards, and when the foot and the toes are brought as nearly as possible into a straight line with the leg.

In lean individuals a line becomes visible between the muscle and the bone in the leg bearing the weight of the body. If it is reproduced in a work of art, care should be taken, at any rate, not to copy its slight irregularities, which arise from unevenness in the anterior edge of the tibia, and by no means add to the beauty of the line. It is better, therefore, to soften them down.

The calf of the male leg should be divided externally, more or less visibly, into three parts, between the hollow of the knee and the heel; the first consisting of the fleshy parts of the gastrocnemius muscle, the second of its broad tendon and the large subjacent muscle of the calf (*M. soleus*), and the third of the common tendon of the two muscles, known as the tendo Achillis, with its insertion into the bone of the heel. This division becomes distinctly marked when the muscles are in action, though it may disappear

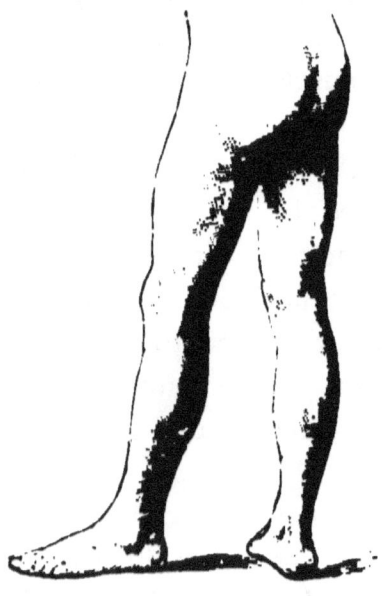

FIG. 29.

completely when they are relaxed. Where the muscles of the calf are not very strongly developed, the division is also incomplete in the ordinary standing attitude, as is seen in Fig. 29, from a photograph from life. One of the legs in the figure illustrates further the bulging of the *tibialis anticus* muscle. In statues the division is generally more distinctly seen in the free leg than in that supporting the body, because in the latter the muscles of the calf are more or less stretched, when, as is usually the case, that leg is resting on the whole surface of the sole of the foot. If, however, a leg is supported on the ball of the foot only, the heel being raised, and at the same time the leg bears any considerable proportion of the weight of the body, or is pressed against the ground during movement, then the divisions become conspicuous.

A similar division is also present in the female calf, though it is less easy to follow in detail than in the male, owing to the layer of fat, which may be regarded as normal in the female body, and in no way detracting from its beauty. Thus a difference arises in the profile outline of the leg in the two sexes. If we imagine the leg of a male figure so placed that the outline of the tendo Achillis forms a vertical line, then at the point where the flat tendon of the gastrocnemius commences it will run a little obliquely backwards, and ascend in that direction, almost in a straight line, to where the tendon passes into the muscles. Then follows the bulging caused by the fleshy mass of the gastrocnemius, and constituting the thickest portion of the calf. If we now figure to ourselves the calf of a woman's leg in the same position, the outline continuous with that of the tendo Achillis will begin its oblique course backwards a little earlier, and then pass without any break into the thickest part of the calf; so that, in this instance, the fleshy portion of the gastrocnemius is only seen to project as such under violent contraction, as, for example, in standing on tiptoe.

The greatest antero-posterior diameter of the calf should be large in proportion to the transverse diameter. Among calves of a proportionate girth it is not easy to find examples in which the transverse diameter is too small in proportion to the antero-posterior diameter. Broad and flat calves are ugly, and characteristic of the lower races. In ideal figures, therefore, they should always be avoided.

The girth of the calf in its largest part should be, at least, equal to the neck in the same figure, and may even exceed it without harm. Indeed, the latter is, in fact, the rule, as has been already stated above, where the muscles of the leg are well developed, and, on the other hand, the neck is good in form and free from defects.

In the feet the instep should face upwards, not obliquely upwards and inwards, as is the case in so-called flat feet, that is, feet in which part of the inside of the sole rests on the ground. In ordinary life a high instep is considered a beauty. The ancients did not give any conspicuous expression to this mark of beauty, and I do not think that any artist of the present day is likely to find occasion for taking a lower standard than that of the ancients in this respect. It is another question whether he should exceed that standard. The figure of Harmony, by the Spanish sculptor, Juste Gandarias, which was exhibited at the Vienna Exhibition of

1882, afforded an instance of its being done. It may well be supposed in this case to have been due to the model, since the feet of Spanish men and women are remarkable for their high instep. It produced rather an impression of genre, but was not altogether unpleasing. Far worse deviations from the antique have been reproduced from the living model.

A frequent defect of the foot, especially when the instep is low, is an excessive length of the heel. The foot is prolonged too far backwards, and the profile of the heel, at the base of the tendo Achillis, becomes unduly concave. This is a defect to be carefully avoided, as it is very ugly, and gives a very common aspect to the foot.

Feet of this kind, with a low instep and long heel, lack, in addition, the hollow required in the sole of the foot ; it may, however, be wanting where the instep and heel are normal, if fat is deposited in excess in the central portion of the sole.

With regard to the length of the toes, opinions are at variance. Some authorities insist that the great toe ought to project furthest, others that it should not project quite so far as the second toe, while others again maintain that the two should be of equal length. It is well known that in antique statues the second toe is usually the longer of the two, while the first is longer in living men. Some persons are of opinion that the latter condition is a consequence of wearing boots and shoes, while

others hold that the longer second toe in the antique
is an artistic figment.   Both are in the wrong.

I once took a mould of the foot of an old man
in whom the second toe was obviously longer than
the first.   The foot rested on a plaster ground ; and
having thus procured a deep impression of the foot,
including the very front of the tips of the toes, I obtained a cast of it.   The distance from the hindermost
point of the heel to the tip of the second toe was
244 mm. ; the distance from the same point to the
tip of the first toe was slightly over 242 mm.   The
distances were very accurately measured with a
sliding measured scale.   If a line be imagined as
drawn through the heel and the middle of the second
toe, and then a plane be raised at right angles to this
line from the tip of the second toe, it would lie at
a distance of over 2 mm. from the tip of the great
toe.   The proportions of the toes in this foot do not
materially differ from those of antique statues, and
yet the man wore ordinary foot-gear from his earliest
youth.

Clearly we have not to deal with external influences
only, but also with personal and racial characteristics.
I recollect a photograph of a poor Fellah girl, in
whom the great toe was conspicuously longer than
the second, and yet she had certainly never worn
shoes of the European pattern, and probably never
any at all.

Next, there can be no question of an artistic fiction
on the part of the ancient sculptors.   An Italian

sculptor has informed me that, though in Italy it is
the exception for the second toe to exceed the first
in length, yet it is not infrequently to be met with.

The only doubt remaining is whether a foot of
this form was actually the prevailing type among the
ancient Greeks and Romans, or whether their sculptors selected it in preference to the ordinary type.
However that may be, an artist is justified in representing the feet so, for it is not his duty to reproduce
the commonest type, but that which he regards as
the most beautiful among the forms actually observed
by him. A projecting great toe, from which the line
of the tips of the toes runs down obliquely to the
smallest, is decidedly ugly.

One of the defects ordinarily produced by wearing
boots is the twisting of the great toe towards the
median line of the foot, and the consequent knotted·
aspect of the joint uniting the great toe to the
metatarsus; another is a crushing together of the
toes in general, and distortion of the last toe,
and sometimes also of the last but one. So, too,
the dryness and the relative leanness of the feet
in men, otherwise well nourished, must often be attributed principally to the foot-gear. We enter the
domain of pathology when we find a foot which is
not set correctly and firmly on the lower leg, or when
the entire sole of the foot does not tread the ground
evenly, but chiefly the inner border of it; the latter
condition, combined with a low instep and obliteration
of the hollow of the sole, may offer the type known

to the surgeon as the *Pes valgus*. It is the same as
that known as flat foot. Indeed, it may be affirmed
that for no part of the body is it so difficult to find
good models as for the foot. We have in our country
scarcely any men who walk barefoot from their youth
upwards in summer and winter alike ; and even were
there any such, their feet, owing to the constant
injuries received, would not replace the antique foot,
which was developed in perfect freedom on the sandal
and yet was protected by it. It is, therefore, ad-
visable for artists to study the foot principally from
the antique, and, when they turn to nature for assistance, to avoid anything which differs markedly from
the antique type.

On the question as to what length of leg is the
most desirable in practice, artists are fairly well
agreed. They say of a male statue or of a male
model, " The centre comes in the right place," meaning thereby that the external point of attachment
of the male organ lies exactly halfway up the entire
figure when standing upright. According as they
wish to represent a figure of more lengthy or more
squat proportions, they lengthen or shorten the legs.

Some of the Italian masters suffered themselves to
be misled by their models into shortening the legs,
with very ungraceful results. The most conspicuous
among them is Giulio Romano. The defect is often
observable in works of his later Mantuan period.* I

* Any one who has not the opportunity of convincing himself
on this point in Mantua should visit the Palazzo Michieli dalle

have several times had occasion to insist on the advantages of Italian over German models; but here mention must be made of the fact that the Italians, like the French, are for the most part short-legged, more so than the English, Germans, Poles, and Southern Slavs. They have also shorter arms; but while the latter·may be regarded as an ornament, the shortness of their legs detracts much from their figures. On the other hand, it cannot be denied that short limbs are more favourably adapted to sculptural treatment than long ones. The latter not seldom look as if the muscles lying under the skin had had to be stretched out in order to fit them to the long limbs.

If models were placed before us with the proportions of the Apollo Belvedere or of the Apoxyomenos, we should certainly regard them as marvels of beauty, provided that they also exhibited the contours of the statues named. But such models are not to be found. In dealing with living examples, we may be quite sure that where the limbs are so long the contours will have suffered.

Women have shorter legs on the average than men, and notice is taken of the fact in works of art. But just as exceptions occur in nature, so art, too, has her exceptions. Examples are not confined to the art

Colonne on the Grand Canal in Venice. Some very beautiful tapestries which hang there were worked from designs by Giulio Romano. Studies for the latter are to be found in the Albertina at Vienna.

of the later renaissance and of the *baroque* style, but
occur also among antique works. A female figure,
therefore, with the average relative lengths of a man
or even somewhat greater, is neither unnatural nor
wanting in beauty. An instance of an ugly short-
legged female figure is to be seen in the frescoes of
the Palazzo Farnese at Rome. She is seated by
Hercules, who is depicted playing on a tambourine,
and she probably represents Omphale. On the other
hand, the Juno in the same mythological series main-
tains the proportions of a tall woman in accordance
with the stature ascribed to her.

When a figure is given relatively short legs, the
limbs must be of a powerful type. It will then, at
least, correspond to what exists normally—viz., the
compact and somewhat squat build of powerful
figures. Such figures may not only have an excellent
effect as caryatides in certain architectural combina-
tions, but may even be the only ones possible when,
by reason of the style of architecture, a long-legged
figure would be quite out of harmony with the whole.
Short-legged figures, however, supported on weak legs,
always have a very unhappy effect. There is a well-
known comic picture representing two frogs fencing
with the foils. If we imagine toads put in the place of
the frogs, the effect would be both ugly and senseless.
A figure resting on legs that are alike short and weak
reminds one of a toad standing upright.

A common defect of the legs, even when otherwise
well-formed and with thighs of a proper length,

consists in the lower leg being too short relatively to the thigh, whereas the opposite scarcely ever occurs in individuals of normal development. Some celebrated antiques far exceed the ordinary dimensions in regard to the relative length of the lower leg : for instance, the Apollo in the Vatican, and the Venus de Medicis in her present form. C. Langer (*loc. cit.*, p. 61) even describes the proportions obtaining in them as unnatural.

On the other hand, a very disagreeable impression is produced when the lower legs of a model, which happen to be relatively too short, are imported into a work of art, as has occasionally been done by some Italian masters.

The artist will do well, in judging of a model, to start from the principle that in the living subject the lower leg may be too short relatively to the thigh, but can never be too long, when the thigh is normally developed and not shortened by any kind of distortion.

CONCLUDING REMARKS.

IF, on glancing back over the foregoing pages, we ask on what the beauty of the human figure depends, the answer is, in the first place, on the skeleton. This must have beautiful proportions; the shape of the individual bones must be normal, and the whole framework free from clumsiness. Above all, the articular ends of the bones must not be marred by thickness, and their angles and edges must not be so conspicuously developed as to interfere with the rhythm of the living form.

Next in importance come the muscles. It is undeniable that no male figure can be beautiful unless it possess a well-developed muscular system ; but the muscles cannot be dispensed with in a female figure either. Only they should not be so conspicuous under the skin as in the male ; and they should be covered by a moderate layer of fat.

Fat alone, however, will give no sculptural forms if the subjacent muscles are poorly developed. This is observable in the arms of many women, in which the muscles are ill developed, either from an inherited disposition, or because the arms have not been sufficiently exercised in youth. When in such cases the arms are filled out by deposit of fat, they never attain the æsthetic beauty of arms that have also well-formed muscles. The difference is even more striking if the whole body is taken into account.

Consequently it can never be said that a body has attained the highest point of its beauty, so long as the muscles are not completely developed. In a man this may be estimated by the force which he can exert. But here we must confine ourselves to tests of strength in which the force of the muscles alone comes into play, and not the weight of the body, since the latter may go on increasing for a long time after the muscles are fully developed.

If we pay attention to these principles, we may take the period between the twenty-fourth and the twenty-eighth years in a man as that in which the development of the muscles is completed. It is a matter of subordinate importance that, if the muscles have not been exercised at an early period, their capacity may by practice be increased even at a later period than that above mentioned. It is less easy to fix a similar period for women, as here our experience is more limited, and only conjecturally can we name the period from the twentieth to the twenty-fourth year as that in which, when the conditions of health are unchanged, the mass of the muscular tissue begins to be stationary.

Again, it is not practicable to extend the period of highest bodily beauty to a later limit, because the form of the breasts begins to deteriorate from the twenty-fourth year onwards, though it frequently commences much earlier.

In the third place, we have to consider the fat. Not only the female body, but the male also, requires a certain amount of fat. I once had an opportunity of seeing a man of herculean build, in whom, nevertheless, the subtegumentary fat was almost wholly wanting. The man was decidedly ugly to look at. Apart from the fact that the proportions of his skeleton were not all that could be desired, and that he was of too sturdy a type, a very unpleasant effect was produced by the way in which the thin skin, unsupported by any fat, was drawn over the huge muscles, while the latter, by their contraction, raised shapeless lumps and ridges, and deep furrows were ploughed between them. A slight covering of fat alone can tone down these features, and give rise to the harmonious forms with which we are familiar in the figures of gods, heroes, and athletes left to us by the ancients.

The outlines, however, which the fat stamps on the form of the body change with the different periods of life. The fatness natural to the infant disappears, as a rule, during the years of rapid growth, so that on the completion of puberty the body is usually poor in fat. When any considerable quantities of fat are present, it is found, for the most part, on the trunk, abdomen, and buttocks, and partly also on the breast and thighs. In both sexes fat is wanting on the arms, though in women especially a considerable quantity is frequently stored up in them later on in life. Whether fatness of the upper arm is merely a consequence of advancing years, or also forms part of the changes to which pregnancy and childbirth give rise, I will not venture to say. Certain it is that it is more often seen in married women than in maiden ladies who are no longer young. When the fat disappears with the prime of life, which, as we all know, by no means invariably happens, it disappears, as a rule, first from the face, from the hands and arms, the buttocks and thighs, later from the legs, and last of all from the trunk. Thin old men often retain considerable masses of fat on the abdomen.

The fourth and last element in the beauty of the figure is the skin. The beauty of a delicate skin is the theme of universal praise; but the artist rejoices not so much in a delicate as in an elastic skin. The extent of the elastic fibres that are buried in the connective tissue of the skin varies with the race and with the individual, and on this it depends whether the skin lies close and fits well, or not. The skin must not be too large for the body, as may happen when people once well nourished fall away.

A very delicate skin, but one easily shifted and therefore imperfectly knit to the substructures, may occasionally render details visible in a very elegant way ; but, as a rule, only a skin that is well knit to the subjacent tissues, and further offers a sufficient elastic resistance, shows off the configuration to advantage. Such a skin has a better effect on the joints, and especially on the form and maintenance of the female breast. It is, indeed, quite intelligible that a somewhat dense and resisting skin must retain the breast in its position better than one that is too thin and loose. It will also delay longer the appearance of the fold under the breast, which ruins it from an artistic point of view. We must, however, also note that the nature of the tissues is a general characteristic of the individual, and therefore we are able, from the nature of the connective tissue of the skin, to infer with some probability that of the remaining connective tissue of the same individual. This, however, is the tissue connecting the mammary gland with the subjacent muscles. When, therefore, the skin is only loosely knit, the mammary gland may also be only loosely attached to the muscles.

It is well known that Turkish dancers, the so-called Almeh, can move their breasts, while keeping the body perfectly still, by contracting in an appropriate manner the great pectoral muscle lying beneath them. But it is also known in the East that not every girl who devotes herself to that profession can learn to perform the feat with the same degree of perfection. Since we might suppose that any one could learn the appropriate action of the muscles, it is not unlikely that this difference in the degree of success attained depends on the firmness with which the mammary gland and the great pectoral muscle are connected.

Throughout this book I have founded my arguments on the principle that the most beautiful among human forms are those that ought to be the subject of artistic reproduction—those, namely, which, in all positions and under every aspect, give the best lines.

This idea also pervaded the art of the classical period, and became part of the general consciousness, more especially in the period which is usually known as that of Praxiteles. Once again, however, in bringing my remarks to a close, I must acknowledge that even ideal art may make other demands and set itself other tasks.

We know—and the fact has been referred to several times in the text—that a figure, not in itself wholly free from defects, may be placed in such an attitude or position that a given defect disappears, either wholly, or at least in a particular view. Apart from this, a less beautiful model may produce a better effect in some particular position and for a special purpose than one to whom we should feel compelled to award the palm if we were considering only which was the more fitted to be reproduced

generally. So soon as a figure ceases to stand alone,
it becomes part of a composition, and then its lines
depend on the remaining lines of the composition,
and must be made to harmonise with them. This
is true of all representations of figures in art, whatever the scale of the work, whether in filling up a
pediment or in beating out an ornament in *repoussé*
work.

INDEX.

Printed by Hazell, Watson, & Viney, Ld., London and Aylesbury.

H. GREVEL & CO.'S PUBLICATIONS.

The Student's Fine Art Library.

THE CLASSICAL PICTURE GALLERY FOR 1891: Monthly Magazine of Reproductions from the Art Galleries of Europe. Each Part 1s., containing Twelve Plates, 4to. Annual Subscription, 14s., post free.

"Judged by their price, the plates are little short of wonderful. They will be of no little value to the serious student of art, who will be able by its means to compare types and expressions, and refresh his memory in various ways."— *Saturday Review*.

THE CLASSICAL PICTURE GALLERY. Annual Volume for 1890, containing 144 Plates. With Biographical Notices of the Artists, and a Complete Index. 1 Vol. 4to, cloth extra, gilt top. £1 1s.

THE HUMAN FIGURE: its Beauties and Defects. By ERNST BRÜCKE, Emeritus Professor of Physiology in the University of Vienna, and formerly Teacher of Anatomy in the Academy of Fine Arts at Berlin. Authorised translation. Revised by the Author. With 29 Illustrations by Hermann Paar. Edited by Prof. W. Anderson, Royal Academy of Arts, London. Crown 8vo, cloth. 10s. 6d.

THE STUDENT'S ATLAS OF ARTISTIC ANATOMY, for the Use of Sculptors, Painters, Medical Students, and Amateurs. With THIRTY-FOUR PLATES. By CHARLES ROTH, Professor of Sculpture at the Munich Academy. Edited by C. E. FITZGERALD, M.D. 1 Vol. Fol., in cloth case. £1 5s.

"A valuable aid to the study of artistic anatomy, and in itself a work of art." —*Lancet*.

DIEGO VELAZQUEZ AND HIS TIMES. By CARL JUSTI, Professor at the University of Bonn. Translated by PROFESSOR A. H. KEANE, and Revised by the Author. With 52 Magnificent Woodcuts, an Etching of Velazquez' Own Portrait by Forberg, and a Plan of the Old Palace at Madrid. 1 Vol. Royal 8vo, Roxburgh. £1 1s.

"No better example could be given of the growth of historical knowledge during the past thirty years than is to be found in Carl Justi's recent book on 'Velazquez,' well translated by Professor A. H. Keane. The amount of research and of real observation which his book shows is typical of the modern cholar."—*Times*.

MANUAL OF ARCHÆOLOGY : containing an Introduction to Egyptian and Oriental Art, Greek, Etruscan, and Roman Art. With 114 Illustrations. By TALFOURD ELY, Member of the Councils of the Society for the Promotion of Hellenic Studies. 1 Vol. Crown 8vo, cloth. 6s.

"A most admirable gift to those who take an intelligent interest in ancient art."—*Graphic.*

MANUAL OF BIBLIOGRAPHY : being an Introduction to the Knowledge of the Book, Library Management, and the Art of Cataloguing. With a Glossary of Technical Terms, and a Latin-English and English-Latin Topographical Index of the Early Printing Centres. With 37 Illustrations. New Edition. By WALTER T. ROGERS, Inner Temple Library. 1 Vol. Crown 8vo, cloth. 5s.

"Contains much rare and curious information."— *Morning Post.*

MANUAL OF MYTHOLOGY IN RELATION TO GREEK ART. By MAXIME COLLIGNON, late Member of the École Française, Athens. Translated and Enlarged by JANE E. HARRISON, Author of "Myths of the Odyssey," "Introductory Studies in Greek Art," etc. With 140 Illustrations. Crown 8vo, cloth extra, gilt top. 10s. 6d.

"This is a good book. It fills a gap in our literature, doing for Greek mythology much the same service which Mrs. Jamieson rendered to Christian hagiology."—*Academy*

MANUAL OF ANCIENT SCULPTURE. By PIERRE PARIS, formerly Member of the École Française, at Athens. Edited and Augmented by JANE E. HARRISON, Author of " Myths of the Odyssey," "Introductory Studies in Greek Art," etc. With 187 Illustrations. Crown 8vo, cloth extra, gilt top. 10s. 6d.

"It is written in a felicitous and interesting style, and its illustrations, numbering in all 187, reproduce in an accurate manner the best of the sculptured treasures which are referred to in the text."—*Scotsman.*

MANUAL OF EGYPTIAN ARCHÆOLOGY. By PROFESSOR G. MASPERO, D.C.L. Oxon. English Edition, with Notes, by AMELIA B. EDWARDS, Ph.D., LL D. With 299 Illustrations. New Edition, revised, with a Complete Index. Crown 8vo, cloth extra, gilt top. 10s. 6d.

CONTENTS.—Chapter I. Civil and Military Architecture. —Chapter II. Religious Architecture.—Chapter III. Tombs.—Chapter IV. Painting and Sculpture.—Chapter V. The Industrial Arts.

"It is a marvel of erudition and condensation. It sums up the long results of thousands of years of Egyptian civilisation in language precise enough to make the work a handbook for the specialist, and popular enough to ensure its becoming a guide to the antiquarian lore of the country for travellers in Egypt." —*Scotsman.*

MANUAL OF ORIENTAL ANTIQUITIES: including the Architecture, Sculpture, and Industrial Arts of Chaldæa, Assyria, Persia, Syria, Judæa, Phœnicia, and Carthage.

By ERNEST BABELON, Librarian of the Department of Medals and Antiques in the Bibliothèque Nationale, Paris. Translated and enlarged by B. T. A. EVETTS, M.A., of the Department of Egyptian and Assyrian Antiquities, British Museum. With 241 Illustrations. Crown 8vo, cloth extra, gilt top. 10s. 6d.

" The *Manual of Oriental Antiquities*, which takes deservedly a high position both for the general accuracy of its statements and the excellent character of its illustrations."—*Athenæum.*

MANUAL OF EMBROIDERY AND LACE: their Manufacture and History from the Remotest Antiquity to the Present Day.

By ERNEST LEFÉBURE, Lace Manufacturer and Administrator of the Musée des Arts Decoratifs, Paris. Translated and Enlarged, with Notes and New Designs, by ALAN S. COLE, of the South Kensington Museum, With 156 Illustrations. Crown 8vo, cloth extra, gilt top. 10s. 6d.

' A book which is not only a comprehensive, well-arranged, and trustworthy history of a delightful art, but a book which is pleasant to see, and pleasant to read, well written and well edited."—*Academy.*

MANUAL OF MUSICAL HISTORY: A Bio-Bibliographical Survey.

With 150 Illustrations of Portraits, Musical Instruments, Facsimiles of Rare and Curious Musical Works. By JAMES E. MATTHEW. 1 Vol. Crown 8vo, cloth. 10s. 6d.

THE STUDENT'S ARCHAEOLOGICAL ATLAS TO HOMER.

Thirty-six Plates with descriptive Text. By Dr. R. ENGELMANN and Prof. W. C. F. ANDERSON. 1 Vol. 4to. Cloth. 10s. 6d.

OLYMPOS: Tales of the Gods of Greece and Rome.

By TALFOURD ELY. With 47 Woodcuts and 6 full-page Photographic Plates. 1 Vol. Crown 8vo, cloth. 10s. 6d.

ARCHITECTURAL MONUMENTS and BUILDINGS of GREAT BRITAIN and IRELAND.

Edited by CONSTANTINE UHDE. In 6 Parts, Fol., containing 150 magnificent Photographs of the most remarkable Architectural Monuments. Each Part £1 5s.

**THE BOOK : its Printers, Illustrators, and Binders,
from Gutenberg to the Present Time.** By HENRI
BOUCHOT, of the National Library, Paris. With a Treatise on
the Art of Collecting and Describing Early Printed Books, and a
Latin-English and English-Latin Topographical Index of the
Earliest Printing Presses. Edited by H. GREVEL. Containing
172 Facsimiles of Early Typography, Book Illustrations, Printers'
Marks, Bindings, numerous Borders, Initials, Head and Tail Pieces,
and a Frontispiece. 1 Vol. Royal 8vo, 383 pages, vellum cloth.
£1 1s. Edition de Luxe, £2 2s.

Beginning with the Block Books, which anticipated by a few decades the
discovery of Printing, this work gives an account of the rise and progress of
Printing, the dispersion over Europe of the German printers, the growth of
Book Illustration, of the Binder's Art, and all similar matter down to the present
day, and serves at the same time as a guide for collecting and describing early
Printed Books.

**RICHARD WAGNER'S LETTERS TO HIS
DRESDEN FRIENDS (Letters to Theodor Uhlig,
1840-1853; Letters to Wilhelm Fischer, 1841-1859;
Letters to Ferdinand Heine, 1841-1868).** Translated
by J. S. SHEDLOCK. With an ETCHING by C. W. SHERBORN
of WAGNER'S PORTRAIT taken in 1853. and a COMPLETE INDEX.
1 Vol. Crown 8vo, cloth extra, gilt top. 12s. 6d.

"Admirer's of Wagner's genius will find here a fund of information about
the *vie intime* of the musician."—*Graphic.*

**CORRESPONDENCE OF WAGNER AND LISZT
FROM 1841 TO 1861.** Translated into English, and with a
Preface by Dr. FRANCIS HÜFFER. 2 Vols. Crown 8vo, cloth,
gilt top. £1 4s.

"Nothing more instructive with regard to the real character and relations
of Liszt and Wagner has been published. Seldom has the force and fervour of
Wagner's German been rendered with such accuracy and character in a strange
tongue."—*Manchester Guardian.*

**THE SWORDSMAN : a Manual of Fence for the
Foil, Sabre, and Bayonet. With an Appendix consisting of a Code of Rules for Assaults, Competitions,
etc.** By ALFRED HUTTON, late Capt. King's Dragoon Guards,
Author of "Cold Steel," "Fixed Bayonets." With 42 Illustrations. 1 Vol. Crown 8vo, cloth. 3s. 6d.
Ditto, 50 copies on Whatman paper, bound in vellum. 10s. 6d.

**PRACTICAL GRAMMAR OF THE GERMAN
LANGUAGE. With Reading Lessons, and a Ger-
man-English and English-German Vocabulary.** By
WILLIAM EYSENBACH. Third Edition. 1 Vol. 8vo, cloth.
3s. 6d.

"It is decidedly '*practical.*' We like its gradual mode of presenting difficulty
after difficulty, and the conversational tone of the exercises."—*Schoolmaster.*

**DICTIONARY OF THE ENGLISH AND GER-
MAN LANGUAGES.** By Dr. FR. KOEHLER. Two Parts in
One Volume. 1 Vol. 8vo, half calf. 7s. 6d.

H. GREVEL & CO., 33, KING STREET, COVENT GARDEN, LONDON. W.C.

www.ingramcontent.com/pod-product-compliance
Lightning Source LLC
Chambersburg PA
CBHW020627030726
47497CB00007B/2442